In *Deep Shade*, Kindred Stockton delivers a mesmerizing, cybernetic, Gnostic soap opera for the vape age. Equal parts haunting and funny, *Deep Shade* reads like a wry meditation on the koan, "Who is the great master who makes the grass green?" I can just picture Alfred Korzybski and Henry David Thoreau discussing the ideas of *Deep Shade* at a Dunkin'-catered interdimensional salon. Stockton expertly weaves a tale with delightful twists and turns, showing the reader time and time again that the map is most certainly not the territory. Stunning debut!

—Brian Jacobson,
author of *The Truth About the Moon and the Stars*

Deep Shade is an absurdity, wrapped in a farce, but it just might be prophetic.

—Jesse McKinnell,
author of *Anarchy and Other Lies*

D1059952

DEEP SHADE

By

Kindred Stockton

MONTAG

Montag Press ISBN: 978-1-940233-92-5
Design © 2021 Amit Dey

Montag Press Team:

Editor: Charlie Franco
Cover: Daniel Morgan

A Montag Press Book
www.montagpress.com
Montag Press
777 Morton Street, Unit B
San Francisco CA 94129 USA

Montag Press, the burning book with the hatchet cover, the skewed word mark and the portrayal of the long-suffering fireman mascot are trademarks of Montag Press.

Printed & Digitally Originated in the United States of America
10 9 8 7 6 5 4 3 2 1

Acknowledgements

Big ups to my editor Charlie Franco, we don't know when he sleeps.

I have to give my sincerest gratitude to everyone who has nurtured my potential from the time I was a little boy.

To my mother, who always encouraged my creative expression.

To my father, who always provided a safe harbor.

To my brother Greg, who showed me something to aspire to.

To my friends, who picked me up and dragged me along on endless adventures, and humored my wild ideas: Alex, Bill, Chris, Dan, Ian, MacBeth, Zak, Gilly, Caleb, Adam St. John, Dave Gunsallus, Nick Maglia, Sam Knowlton, Sean Mullins, Jesse Rogers, and many more kindred spirits.

To all my teachers:

Tena Ruby, with her seemingly inexhaustible patience.

Patrick Allen, who crushed a tic tac container underfoot in 6th grade and had us imagine the shards as pieces of a story.

Madame Mikan, who always kept her sense of humor intact and whose creative writing club kept the flame alive.

To Sean Smith, the real life Ralph Burgman. You taught me to wield a chainsaw, and your unsurpassed professionalism made you a great mentor. You always kept us safe in the woods, and tried mightily to keep us awake in the truck.

And to my beautiful wife Moira, whose love and support made this possible.

From the bottom of my heart: thank you. You all have made me the man I am today.

This novel is dedicated to the starry-eyed dreamers waking up in New Atlantis.

CHAPTER 1

Ain't nobody slowing down no way,
Everybody's stepping on their accelerator.

—The Rolling Stones, *Ventilator Blues*

A coffee cup tossed from the DVO lane tumbled across the line dividing driverless vehicles and piloted vehicles and flittered down into the gutter of the highway. A small recycling drone sucked it up and whirred onwards in the margin. Someone braked to watch it happen.

Auto-piloted cars whizzed past Aaron Waters' vehicle. The life he had imagined was also passing him on the left in the "Driverless Vehicles Only" lane but at least he was still moving.

Aaron was late to work again and couldn't afford to be caught behind someone slow, run out of fuel, or have his motor overheat. He checked the engine temperature and fuel level on the dash and looked up to see brake lights alarmingly close. With a tinge of adrenaline, his leg jerked onto the brake pedal and the mechanism in the seat belt locked. The car squealed to a halt and stalled out. The DVO lanes were humming merrily along.

If I ever win the lottery, Aaron thought to himself, *I wouldn't even sell this piece of junk. I'll just leave it here on this highway to rot and order a driverless delivered.* He turned the key and the un-killable little 0.5-L engine fired right up. Aaron accelerated as quickly as his 20-year-old Honda Squire would allow.

He rolled down his window thinking about a cool breeze but thought better of it as a blast of fumes and asphalt radiation engulfed the car's interior. Cranking the fan caused something in there to rattle, reminding him the A/C didn't work and he couldn't afford to fix it on his wage from working as an environmental technician. He glanced at the motor temp gauge and hoped it would keep pointing down the middle. He didn't want to have to turn on the heat to cool the engine. *God,* he half-prayed, *please make the coolant system endure this highway.*

Meanwhile, a bit of heat drifted inside a cool, climate-controlled cabin of a Ford A-250 before the computer sensed the change and rolled up the window. A dew of sweat had already formed on the forehead of its owner, the litterbug, who was relieved when the climate bubble stabilized. They began to feel drowsy despite their piping hot coffee.

Funny how sometimes a coffee will put you to sleep! the occupant of the luxury truck thought to themself. *Look at all those poor souls in the Piloted Vehicles Only lane. How sad,* the litterbug pretended to empathize, *they have to just sit there because someone decided to brake for some silly reason or another.* Their cars flashed past soundlessly behind glass and metal and symbolically by the money it takes to purchase such a position. Up ahead in the DVO lane, an automatic fuel delivery truck was restricting traffic to driving at the 120-mph speed limit for hazardous materials.

Aaron Waters' vehicle barely functioned through the stop-and-go traffic all the way to his job. Walking up the gravel lot to the garage of the state vehicles and equipment, almost too late, Aaron found his co-workers already completing the morning inspections of their brushing armor.

The armor suits kept the big branches and tiny shards of fiberweed from bludgeoning or piercing the occupant's body. They also leaked poison juice. Aaron recalled the word *phytophototoxin*. After a day in the sun and dusty wind, traversing the barren countryside and wielding the huge diesel brush arm, the operator would be drenched. The juice reeked like lettuce and dirty laundry and when the sun hit the sap on your skin it made it blister. If you hit a giant grasshopper with the brush arm, the slimy green blood and guts caked on in the sun and wouldn't scrub off even with the pneumatic wire brushes.

Aaron's supervisor, Ralph Burgman, shook his head from the driver's seat as Aaron approached the work truck late again, and then looked back down at an info stream on the console of the Department of Permaculture's newish A-550. The truck was capable of carrying 6 workers while hauling their gear: 4 suits of armor, brush arms, and the fuel toter parked in the bed. Driverless navigation didn't work on the dirt roads that the crew took to their work, so Ralph turned a switch on the dashboard into manual navigation.

They rotated which member of the crew got the special responsibility of driving the fuel toter and listening to the drones on the radio for potential hazards, but if you were late, you lost your chance. As he walked in shame toward the group at a steady pace, Aaron knew that today he wouldn't be driving the toter.

"What's a matter, Aaron? Your holographic girlfriend keepin' you up too late?" Pete Barbour, his only real chum on the crew, said as he addressed him.

"Yeah, what's up Waters, you plugged into the pornograph too long or what?" Joey Dimanche, a greenhorn from Clearwater, projected at Aaron.

Aaron felt the anger bubble up inside like the opening of a shaken three-liter bottle of Coke on a hot afternoon. He struggled to come up with a response and the anger melted into sadness. His tiredness was following him. He felt as if an additional lead weight had been tacked onto his belt loop at the end of every day for the last few years running. And even though it was all his fault, somehow he wanted to put that weight on everyone else around him.

"I just can't --" *Can't what?* He thought to himself.

"Can't what? Can't never make it to work on time? Yeah, we know, asshole," the machined metal voice of Mark Bulkowitz came laughing out of the cybernetic helm of the brushing armor system.

He was a real dirt bag, running his helm for fun before he had to put it on for work.

"Can't keep doing *this*. Working for next to nothing, doing a thankless job, grinding just to make another dinner and fall asleep, only to wake to this again. But I can't afford not to. Look at my hands! Peeling to the pulp. What is this all even for?"

"'All in the service of Capital," Mark said either sarcastically or ironically, Aaron couldn't tell.

"Don't spout that bullpiss here, Bulkowitz. It's too god-damn early," Pete jumped in, equipping his boots and rusted mesh pants.

Pete saw the same unfairness the rest of them did. Even so, there's only so much time a man can think about how bad he's got it at work every day. And anyway, they were all in the same boat. He went on:

"Can't you see it's wrong to only focus on pay? How about some new fuckin' armor? We have helmets that control our minds but we can't get a new pair of boots? And I still have to pay the public fuel tax on the fiberweed ethanol I help to produce. There's no justice anywhere, man."

"It all goes to the same place. We might as well just argue for longer leashes and bigger cages," Aaron said gloomily.

"It's gonna be a scorcher, boys ... it's already muggy and the sun is just above the fiber. Keep up on your hydro levels!" Joey jumped in.

Joey was in high spirits. He had been selected to drive the toter unit which meant he'd be able to rattle off tidbits in the ears of whoever was actually listening to their helm radio. Most of them modded it to run augments and make the time pass. Often when Joey was on the toter it was just him tattling along to himself.

"Shut the fuck up, Joey," Bulkowitz said, which was what Aaron was thinking.

"Which aug' are you gonna run today, Bulkowitz?" Joey replied, patronizing himself.

"Psychedelic Atmosphere 3, I guess," Bulkowitz said mechanically shrugging from inside his armor suit.

A power shrug.

"Psych Atmo sucks... I don't run that joint at all anymore. You should try Rhyme Time."

"Y'all kids're gonna fry your brains runnin' those stupid programs," Pete said as the lone voice of reason through their raging insanity.

"Fry your brains or get your ass canned," crew leader Burgman called back from the truck listening to the conversation.

Pete worked without the radio on. Doing so endangered himself less, he reasoned, than if he had to listen to the anger-provoking insights of one Joey Dimanche.

"I don't know how you operate a brush suit without augmented reality. I would kill myself after a day of that," Joey remarked loud enough for the rest of the crew to hear the youth in his cracking voice.

Aaron threw on his gear without checking it while the tiresome exchange continued. Every day, the same antagonizing and vitriolic nonsense. He'd had enough of the whole dynamic, which was a dangerous attitude considering they were responsible for one another's safety in such a remote and dangerous occupation. He felt trapped in a double-bind, the only exit was a worse impoverishment suckling government cheese while waiting in the labor queue for a new position or perhaps a gnarly and bitter end in the fiber seas of South Florida. Maybe the latter was not so unlikely since he had long ago stopped checking his equipment in the morning in order to make up for his constant late arrivals.

A moment later the work truck was packed with its gear and crew and the toter was hitched. The FM radio spewed unsolicited nonsense in the background as the crew leader stopped scrolling through his tracer feed and put the truck in the manual 'drive' position.

> *"Zero dollars down! Get one for nothing AT ALL!! Buy now, save, and pay later! YOU CAN'T AFFORD IT, BUT YOU NEED IT! Interest may vary, dependenton credit approval, deathiscertain, death and taxes, consult your deity for actual terms and conditions…"*

Aaron was just starting to doze off as his supervisor started their pre-action lecture.

"We need to focus on being thorough today," Burgman said as he addressed his crew and turned down the advert from the driver's seat:

"Leaving stands of fiber behind will attract illegal harvesters, so get 'em all. It doesn't matter how long it takes, it's not a marathon. And if you see anything funny out there, report it. Since that new law, y'all been hearing about passed we could all get fired if one of you sees something and you don't report it. I've even heard that the department is out planting false alarms just to see if we'll report it. Buck told me there was a crew out of Spring Hill that didn't report a fake brush camp on the way to their work site and they all got fined, canned, and now they're due up in court to see if any of them'll serve time. 'Course it could just be Buck trying to scare us with made-up stories," Burgman said mostly to himself as the crew either slept with their eyes open or had headphones in. Except for Joey Dimanche who nodded attentively from the passenger seat.

The truck crawled along the old logging road and Aaron again began to fall asleep like the others. Questions always popped up in his head as he began to doze. *Why do we still call them logging roads if there will never be any more logging?*

Then he was suddenly curious about life in that clandestine brush camp. Never having to go to work, just catching your food and making shelter. Then he thought about eating roasted giant grasshoppers and boiled fiber weed tubers for breakfast, lunch, and dinner. Still, at least no one told them what to do – not until the State of Florida EnCon cops showed up. He drifted further. Morsels of expensive food seemed to hover over him as he dreamed lightly. He was sleeping yet awake. He'd skipped breakfast and now fried coconut shrimp danced above his mouth, just out of reach. Fruit punch seemed to wash over him as the interior of the truck was replaced by a darkened void, silent and velvety.

WHOMP!

The truck hit a pothole and Aaron woke in a daze of hunger and dizzy confusion. Conversations were happening around him and the radio was still on. He felt alone. Fuzz in the peripherals of his vision finally yielded with a yawn and he accepted this reality as current. It was good timing because the truck was just pulling off the dirt road to where they had left off working the day before. It was never pleasant to wake up on arrival at a work site, so at least he had a moment to collect himself before they parked.

Moments later, the crew gathered around the canopied bed of the truck and grabbed their brush arms and helms. The arms each weighed over 100 pounds but the mechanical armor suits bore the brunt of the weight. Aside from the exhaust fumes, which would gather if the crew moved too slowly or if the breeze blew in from behind them, the power suits were incredibly easy to operate. The helms were sealed and climate-controlled, but the exhaust from the suits still managed to get in somehow. The helms showed their coordinates from various geo-stationary GPS satellites. An artificially intelligent voice, if not augmented too much with one of the many mods, reminded them to stay focused on their work and to work safely. To buy one of the suits new would cost the department one whole crew's pay for a year, so they never got new units and their now-ancient suits were noisy and tired. One day every week was devoted to their cleaning and maintenance and there even used to be a weekly safety checklist but it had long since been thrown to the wayside.

Joey, manning the toter, meticulously poured fuel into each crewman's fuel pack which was located on their backs, and then helped connect the fuel lines to the brush arms. The helms turned on automatically when equipped with the AI voice asking if the operator was ready to engage the suit. Except every time Joey's would sing "Are you ready to get shreddy?" and Bulkowitz' would ask "Is it time to party, sir?" Pete's only augment was a music module and Aaron ran no augs at all because he didn't want to get in trouble. The brushing crew took off on foot down the road to where the previous day's mulch heaps yielded to the canes of grassy fiberweed. Joey rolled merrily along behind them in the toter.

"This is the morning radio check. Dimanche to Burgman."

"Burgman. Loud and clear, Joey."

"Dimanche to Waters."

"Waters."

"Dimanche to Barbour."

"Barbour."

"Dimanche to Bulkowitz."

"..." the radio clicked.

"Bulkowitz, please respond."

"Suck my ass, Joey," Bulkowitz said in a direct message to Joey D.

"... Okay. Joey Dimanche to regional. We have four workers on the Six Road north towards Coral Spring, marker three. Three brushers and one toter. Estimated coverage two miles west and one north."

"Dimanche, it's Buck D'Aster at regional HQ. You have clearance to engage. Heat index is Severe. Be safe out there."

The heat index, HI, went from Mild to Moderate to Severe, Extreme, and finally Fatal. In Fatal HI it was impossible for the suits to cool themselves and the operators were at immediate risk of serious injury or death.

"D'Aster, it's Dimanche. Engaging."

In alternating fits of harmony and dissonance, the blare of the engines began to fill the desolate wilderness. The first bristling fiberweed stalk hulking 30 feet high and 6 inches thick at the base was obliterated and spit out by the brush arm of Bulkowitz, who experienced a dazzling myriad of colors and sounds in a kaleidoscope filling his helmed head with augmented reality pleasure.

"I love this shit," he muttered into the private crew radio channel he'd created to exclude Joey.

Rank herbage was ripped and torn from the ground, masticated in the great radial teeth of the brush arms, and fell finally as mulch behind the crew. Joey rolled along over the steaming mulch piles in the 6-wheeled toter. As he lurched along, he vaporized non-intoxicant cannabis extracts with a lithium-ion vaporizer pen. The humidity of the fresh mulch closed in around him and he could feel the sweat dripping down his back. He wished the State of Florida would buy them a newer toter model with a better A/C unit. He took a draw from his vape pen and blew out the turfy exhaust.

If he wasn't careful, which Joey generally wasn't, he could get the toter stuck. Ropy mulch shreds from the towering fiberweed would bind the drive shaft or clog the wheel wells and he'd have to crawl out under there and cut it loose. Preparedness wasn't one of the sorts of things that entertained Joey's mind, but he did carry a knife because he thought it was cool. He would drive the toter without anxiety or regard, blundering along over every pile of shredded vegetation.

CHAPTER 2

They took all the trees
And put 'em in a tree museum
And they charged the people
A dollar and a half to seem 'em

—Joni Mitchell, *Big Yellow Taxi*

The annihilation of the American forest started with the chestnut blight. Vast stands of hulking, provident chestnuts were logged before they could wither and die. The grand symbol of sylvan wildness was reduced to wispy sprouts in the blink of an eye. The rest of the trees hung on much longer as armies of gypsy moths, borers, beetles, and leaf miners wore them down year after year. The ash trees were the first to go, with the oaks and maples taking up the mantle behind them. The pines and other evergreens were leveled with a one-two punch of insects and fire, the fiberweed quickly overtaking their habitat. After the evergreens fell to the weed, the remaining hardwoods were logged off preemptively. The weed deployed itself immediately after that.

Scientists didn't agree on what had caused or created the fiberweed bloom. Some thought it was a random mutation of the domestic bamboo plant that had been granted almost supernatural attributes. Others speculated about genetic engineering and plants modified in secret that had gone wild. Genetic mods had admittedly become ubiquitous.

Genetically modified corn sugar, synthetic protein blends, and even lab-meats had long-ago become the backbone of the federally-subsidized breadbasket of the greatest nation, the United States of America. Thankfully the fiberweed had not yet developed resistance to the proprietary blend of herbicides that were used to secure the corn crop every year. Without those controls, the whole agricultural house of cards would come crashing down.

Whatever its ultimate origin, the obnoxious weed had succeeded in completely suffocating the once-large tracts of diverse forest that had blanketed most of North America and had rendered organic human involvement with any other plant life rather pointless. The great subterranean tubers of the weed sent out runners in every direction, quickly taking over lawns and gardens and every crack of pavement in between. However, nice residential and commercial lawns could still be maintained with the proper growth-reducing inhibitors and almost daily mowing. The fibrous weed itself made for a decent lawn if it was well maintained. But if left to seed the great grassy mats, which had been determined with genetic analysis to be clones of one single plant, would release clouds of pollen and fluffy white seed spawn for miles and miles. It was a glorious gridlock of grass as far as the eye could see. To humans, the rising fiber sea was like what a lawn must be to the tiny ants. And every year it had to be cut, poisoned, and mulched, or else be allowed to bind the land in its green grasp into perpetuity.

After years of spraying the weed with increasingly toxic herbicides and of digging it out, and burning it off, evidence came rolling in that the weed had adapted by growing faster and stronger. What had started as a slight nuisance was almost certainly nudged along by degrees into a disaster by good intentions.

The Florida Department of Permaculture was just in its infancy and at that time widely considered to be an absurd addendum to the increasingly redundant USDA Forest Service. With no forests left, there wasn't a whole lot of forest services needed. It was then that a small number of DoP employees had stepped up and presented a modest solution. The plant was great at sequestering the sun's energy in the form of carbon and it tended to flash into wildfires around October if left alone to dry. So perhaps, they reasoned, it should be collected and used to produce fuel. Fast forward a couple of decades and the chemical energy of the plant concentrated above ground in its stalky, poisonous verdure was routinely harvested by crews who came to the fiberweed first to level the stuff and then later to collect the fermenting piles for processing.

The expense of harvesting that much material was immense at first and until the operation was up and running for long enough to root out the inefficiencies, the Florida DoP fiberweed program was both nationally criticized and almost shut down on multiple occasions. It had taken some dedicated employees years of experimentation by brewing and blending the all-natural fuel in their garages. Gradually these unlikely bureaucrat scientists were able to use their own biofuel to mitigate fuel costs. Soon they had covered all of the Department's expenses and were making money for the State of Florida, but not by a very wide margin. Having proved the concept, they finally won a federal grant and built a state-of-the-art processing facility. The amount of fuel they were producing was still only a drop in the bucket of national demand. Most fuel still flowed down from the great fleet of rigs stationed at the Arctic Sea. But the weed-fuel program soon became the flagship endeavor of the newly formed Florida Department of Permaculture, and most importantly it had gained a foothold. The weed-fuel program, the Department reasoned, was a closed-loop system and it appeared to be sustainable unto perpetuity. As long as there was the fiberweed, the program would continue to maximize its extraction of fuel and money.

Seeing this success, the weed-fuel ideologues at the Department of Permaculture were emboldened. They had seen that their discoveries had now secured a source of revenue and thus a raison d'être. And with that they would embark on the most ambitious engineering project in the history of modern civilization: to rid the atmosphere of centuries of emissions from burnt carbon-based fuel, lower the growing global temperatures, and reverse the rising of sea level. But the ethanol they were producing was itself carbon-based. Buck D'Aster, who'd been around in the early days of the DoP, had often told his favorite crew leader Ralph Burgman (and anyone else who would listen) that it would never work.

"You can't put that genie back in the lamp," he would say. The Department never spent any money on wage increases, and though Burgman's crew had just gotten a new truck it was the only new equipment in recent memory. For this reason, everyone assumed there was already some big expensive plan in the works to remove atmospheric carbon. Aaron would think about it sometimes. *How can you take energy-depleted carbon dioxide out of the atmosphere?*

Every solution Aaron thought of as to how to achieve the stated program goals was either carbon neutral or used more energy and thus released more carbon than it removed. The only idea he had come up with which unequivocally put carbon away was to turn as much of the fiberweed as possible into charcoal and to bury it. But if they buried it, they wouldn't get the money from turning it into fuel and the harvest would become *financially* unsustainable, which everyone knew was much worse than being ecologically unsustainable. *There's gotta be someone smarter than me working on this,* he had reasoned to himself. *Or maybe Buck is right; maybe it just can't be done.*

But Aaron knew one thing; if anyone figured it out, they would get rich like the early developers of the fiberweed ethanol program. Those people were all at least commissioners now, and no one who worked in the fiberweed ever saw them out in the field anymore. All except Buck, who didn't seem to be rich and who would occasionally leave the safety and comforts of the office to see how his crews were faring in the heat.

CHAPTER 3

"There are periods of history when the visions of madmen and dope fiends are a better guide to reality than the common-sense interpretation of data available to the so-called normal mind. This is one such period, if you haven't noticed already."

–Robert Shea and Robert Anton Wilson,
The Eye in the Pyramid

Aaron grappled with his brush arm as he struggled to hold his balance. It felt to him as if the stumps of fiberweed were jumping out in an attempt to trip him and he stumbled a bit before engaging a small stand to level it. He exhaled and his helm alerted him in the default calm, feminine voice:

"Sensors show that you are low on electrolytes, Aaron. Please consider taking a break to hydrate and eat a salt biscuit."

He knew this warning meant his suit would force him to take a break soon so Aaron took a seat on a warm mulch pile. He watched the others go on ahead. He wondered how they managed to stay motivated day in and day out, mile after mile, acre after acre of brushing down fiberweed. He knew about the fuels production game and how homegrown fuels were being lionized in the media. But he didn't personally benefit from that, other than when the occasional stranger bought him a beer at the bar when they found out what he did for a living. His compensation for working for the State of Florida Department of Permaculture Fiberweed Division was not much more than the federal minimum wage of C75.76 an hour and it wasn't nearly enough to start a family or even live with dignity. Whereas a lot of the people he had gone to school with were getting salaries at the Big Info firms. He would often imagine them sitting there in their air-conditioned boardrooms, bullshitting about trends and topics for other minds to consume. It didn't seem like something he'd prefer over splintering fiber stands, but with that kind of Carbon he would have been able to afford a driverless vehicle and it wouldn't have even mattered. *What a way to go*, he thought, *sitting around all day, getting rides, getting fed.*

"Hey Waters, you good?" Joey radioed privately, as the youth came bopping along presently upon the toter.

Joey always had a way of turning up at just the wrong time. Right when Aaron seemed to be getting his mind ordered, the new kid comes along to interrupt his stream of thought. He looked up, took off his helm, and his thoughts involuntarily materialized into words:

"Damn it, Joey. No. I'm not good. This job is killing me. I don't know why I keep doing this except that I need the money for rent and food."

Aaron didn't mean to take it out on him, but Joey didn't seem offended.

"It's not that bad. At least we get out of the city plus we get to see this glorious countryside. And just think of all the fuel this crap is going to make. That's what keeps me going, and this," Joey said and handed Aaron his vape pen and half-smiled.

"Nicotine? I don't do tobacco."

"No, Cannabidiol. CBD. And other cannabis extracts. Totally legal, it won't get you stoned or arrested," Joey spoke fast and breathed deeply, youthfully exuberant about sharing his secret.

Aaron raised it to his eye and read the side of the small metal cylinder:

> GUMMY NUGS *Juice Cake*™: *a MonDow*© *prod-*
> *uct.* "The function is in the flavor." *This product*
> *meets the requirements for sale in the U.S. and Canada.*
> *Only legal cannabis extracts. Don't use this product if*
> *pregnant or nursing.*

"I don't know, Joey. I've never even heard of this stuff. Does Burgman know you're taking this stuff while driving the toter?"

"I'm not!" the boy lied stupidly. "Besides, it doesn't do anything really. Just tastes good and makes your headaches go away."

"Alright, why not?" Aaron said, realizing he just didn't care enough to argue with anyone anymore.

Plus, he was starting to think that he could feel like maybe he could sense a headache might be coming on, which in all honesty was probably just the hydro-electrolyte-deprivation that his brush helm had warned him about. He pressed the red button on the vape tube and a cheap whistling sound effect startled him. The gizmo in his hand began to leak silvery-white vapor in snaky swirls, so he pressed his lips to it as if it was a straw. The vapor he inhaled was cool and tasted like ripe strawberry and melon, and when he exhaled through his nostrils, he gathered hints of banana as well. The aftertaste was green and savory, like how he remembered fresh-cut lawns from when he was a kid. Immediately he sensed the stress melting off his shoulders. The light of the sun seemed friendly instead of oppressive. He smiled and took another big whiff.

"Alright, hey! Those cartridges aren't cheap," Joey told him, reaching for the vaporizer.

And they sat there for a moment, Aaron on the warm fiberweed mulch and Joey on the toter. The sun was baking the mulch, issuing fermenting vegetal warmth up from the ground.

"Where do you get those things?" Aaron asked, after a spell.

"Luke's on 5th Ave. in Tampa. 400 carb including tax, cash only. They're new, it's probably why you've never heard of them, made right in St. Pete."

"400? That's pretty steep, how many puffs do you get off one?"

"I don't know, twenty? We should get back to it; I can't even hear those guys anymore. They're ripping!"

A linear stand of fiberweed 50 yards across stretched out into the distance and around the hillside. Pete and Bulkowitz had leveled their stands to the left and right of it, literally leaving Aaron's work cut out for him. Their helms were pro-grammed to ensure workers had equal work for the day. This meant the fast ones sat in the air-conditioned truck while the slow ones continued their work.

"Drink some hydro. How's your fuel?" Joey demanded, tossing a sealed water pack to him.

" Low. Hit me."

Joey connected the line from the toter to Aaron's back. Aaron consumed the water pack and put his helm on. He could see the fuel level rising and the line of vegetation in front of him was illuminated in slow pulses by the default reality augmentation. After the vape hit, it no longer seemed like such a daunting task.

"There. You should be good for a while. I'm going to catch up with the others and see if they need anything. Call me if something comes up. And be careful out there, it's starting to get hot. Don't work too fast!" Joey called out as he bumbled on by, tromping over the shreds in the toter. Briefly, two spirals of vape exhaust gracefully followed him and disappeared in the heat.

Aaron engaged his brush arm and made his way to where he had left off. He watched as the stalks were drawn in and transformed into blankets of dust and splinters at the tips of his fingers. He imagined the brush arm as an extension of his body. Slowly it dawned on him the power that he had been wielding mindlessly all this time. He thought, *This must be how a hurricane feels.*

And what a strange thought, indeed. He lucidly thought about the thought itself, as he continued to destroy the stalks of messy green and yellow. Despite this new sense of awe and wonder, he began to feel dread once more about what he was doing with his life. But this feeling dwelt only in the periphery because he was having fun in trying to see how quickly and thoroughly, he could level the burly, resilient plants.

At some point, the sound of silver bells started to chime to him, and growing in volume, played to him in a disconcerting way. A sudden vertigo summoned Aaron to check his body's hydro-level displayed on his helm screen and he noted with relief that it lay in the green. Green checks also accompanied every physical assessment: blood pressure, heart rate, and body temp. He was going hard but still feeling good. Mentally he wasn't sweating it either; it felt like week-two instead of year-two on the job. *This is too easy,* he thought. *What was that chiming though? Was it just a side-effect of puffing on that Gummy Nugs© vaporizer or what?* He pressed on.

And that's when he encountered the entity; or rather sensed its presence. He bumble-nudged the form with his brush arm with a slight *Thwack.* The brush arm, glancing off a solid object, sprayed matter and almost stalled the motor. Looking up, Aaron found himself standing before a huge mass. The gravity of it outweighed all the previous brush. It was ten or even 100 times the size of any of the fiberweed stalks. Shaded from the sun, Aaron was suddenly transported to one of his childhood memory implants: Selling Summer's Lemonade and Riding Bikes Up and Down the Street. It was an Oak Tree. *That was one of my favorite memories!* He thought. He thought about that thought as it slowly dawned on him that the memory wasn't real. It was just a virtual reality dream from a VR lesson administered by the school in his home regional settlement. He had never seen a real Oak. Not until now.

Aaron laughed and thrust himself down, powering off his equipment. He took off his helm in the deep shade and wondered. Wondered what to do now. Wondered how this thing got here. The required modus operandi had always been clear: turn *any* vegetation into mulch. Be the destroyer upon the landscape. And now this giant 'Tree' stood to him, a good 4 feet across and at least 75' tall, just bristling with dissonant harmony. He was physically barred from going forward with his assigned cut.

He deliberated whether he was hallucinating. He bent down and sniffed at the cut that his brush arm made in the trunk. It was a deep and musky smell, unlike the fetid lettuce odor of the fiberweed mulch. His eye gravitated to a small movement on the bark. It was a fly, a strange gold little fly with green eyes. It was hovering in one place. And then it was gone. He closed his eyes and heard distant chimes. He could've dozed off if a barky scraping hadn't made him start.

Something was skittering about on the trunk a few meters up. There was something alive, chirping at him. A wild critter, a squirrel? He hadn't seen one of those in forever, not since the field trip to the zoo in 8th grade. It whipped its tail at him, warning him. He laughed and it did him a world good. *Such a little thing pretending such ferocity. Where the heck had it come from?* Only the fabulously wealthy had access to wild animals in their strictly maintained hunting and leisure preserves. Anyone who had tasted wild meat other than grasshopper was certainly in a minority; most had only ever had the cheap and plentiful gen-mod lab meat products. There just wasn't anything like this left.

"Dimanche to Waters," Aaron's discarded helm verbalized remotely.

"Hey, Joey!" Aaron replied, wondering if his response was too enthusiastic.

"Hey, what is your ETA to the rally point?"

What should I tell him? That I'm not going because I found a miracle?

"I'm not – ah, I don't know."

"What do you mean 'you don't know'? What's your helm say!?" Joey sounded off impatiently.

Aaron imagined the rest of the crew waiting for him, having finished their work. All tuned out in the truck, looking at their tracer feeds. Burgman cursing him out and wishing he hadn't hired him. And again, he laughed.

"Joey, I took my helm off," Aaron spoke at the helm on the ground.

"What? Why!?"

How would he explain this? He thought about it some as the ethereal shade dappled across his forehead. He felt his weight gradually ease into the trunk of the Tree. He clutched at the ground and picked up a small funny-looking object. *What were those things called? Corn nuts? Acorns.* He slipped one into his pocket. A breeze tossed the living leaves around into a chorus of white noise and he began to snooze. He might've heard bells tingling as his lights went out. There he slumbered better than he had in two years.

CHAPTER 4

Also Brought to You by ADVISO®!! ... the
Ad Visor™ that Delivers Ads — and Carbon! —
Directly to You and Your Friends 'n' Family

They found him lying in a stand of mature fiberweed five meters off the mulch field, helm off and severely dehydrated. It had been over an hour since his last radio contact, though the crew had naturally stood around for another 25 minutes before actually trying to go and find him. He wasn't difficult to find even in the remote wilderness of the fiber barrens, for the helms had radio tracking chips. An incident report was filed and notarized even before he was released from the emergency medical clinic.

Getting out of the clinic was easier than getting in. It was inside a complex of other medical specialists and clinics, so naturally, it took 30 minutes to ascertain that all they needed was the correct information on their paperwork. And all the hospital reception office needed for the information to be correct was for Ralph Burgman to have his crew leader's medical incident ID card. But that had never been issued so Ralph had to trace the Department of Permaculture's health and safety person and get it issued. All they had to do was create a holographic copy and send it, and that only took them another 30 minutes. Finally, they were cleared to get Aaron looked at, once they knew the State would be on the hook for the bill. The simple reception droid spat out a packet for Aaron and his crew leader Ralph.

"Always reject the arbitration provision," Ralph Burgman advised to his crewmember, remembering something Buck D'Aster had told him years ago.

"I reject the arbitration provision," Aaron told the mechanical administrator drone handling their case.

The droid took a moment to process the information and printed out the new forms.

Aaron looked at Ralph as he was reaching for the forms. His hands wavered because the drone held onto the papers for a moment before releasing them. Aaron trusted Ralph a great deal and wished he could be a better employee. *Why couldn't he?* There was something in the way, a metaphorical oak in the path.

At first, it seemed to the nurses and doctors to be a simple case of heat exhaustion and hallucination. No one actually believed Aaron's story about how he saw a Tree in the wild. It had been a decade since the last wild hardwoods had been cut for high-end flooring and veneer, and luxury artisanal firewood. Now the only large trees that existed were in the private cities, in their guarded arboretums. Everyone knew that.

It was a cut and dry case ... at first. Then they discovered the acorn.

They found it right on the bed where he was resting with an IV in his arm. The nurse that discovered it had never seen one. A doctor of authority was called in, Dr. Eddy Horn. He was older than the nurses and could recall such oddities being much more common. Everyone involved wondered if heat stroke was the correct diagnosis. After all, what if he *had* seen an Oak out there?

Aaron's supervisor, Ralph Burgman, was called in to examine the acorn and answer some questions Dr. Horn had about the whole situation.

"You say your guys found him out in the brush, right? And there definitely wasn't an Oak Tree nearby? What are the odds he's putting us on? Do you have video surveillance outfitted with any of your equipment?" The doctor asked as he pressed the crew supervisor relentlessly to get to the heart of the story.

"Just laying there in the fiberweed, no trees for miles and miles. Aaron doesn't have much of a sense of humor either. He's kind of a quiet guy, most of the time. Unfortunately, we don't have any cameras on the equipment, only on the truck," he lied. "But we have the coordinates of where he stopped. Why?" Ralph asked the doctor.

"Interesting…"

"What's going on?"

"We found this…" Dr. Horn said as he held out the acorn for Burgman to see.

"What the hell? Well, guess I've gotta call this in and do the paperwork for that, too. A heat-related injury and an antiquities discovery, all in one day: this day is getting a little too interesting," the crew leader intoned.

Burgman wandered outside to trace his superiors at the department and report the news. The Tree, if they could find it, would undoubtedly bring in a lot of money, which they could use for replacing old mulch harvesters. Those darn things were always breaking down in the most inconvenient locations.

Meanwhile, Dr. Horn checked in with his patient. First, he dismissed the nurses, who were happy to get out for a smoke break and talk about whatever else besides work.

"How are we feeling, Mr. Waters?" the doctor asked, lightly patting his shoulder.

"Just fine. A little tired, I guess. Long day." Aaron replied.

"We need to know some details about this long day of yours. Specifically, we need to know the last thing you remember before you fainted out there," the doctor spoke slyly.

Aaron thought, *there's never been a doctor that has shown any interest in me before...*

"Well, I just remember cooling off in the shade of that huge Tree. There was a squirrel, and–"

"A squirrel? You don't say.... And it was outside of a preserve? Incredible! Most people haven't seen a real one, they think the android ones they stock in the parks are real, but of course, they aren't," the doctor explained with apparent condescension.

"Yeah. I remember I grabbed the acorn, heard some bells, and then just fell asleep. I dreamt about a big plate of spaghetti and meatballs."

"Bells... interesting."

Doctor Horn stroked the white stubble on his face. He hadn't believed the young man's story until this point. He still didn't fully believe it, but the significance of this case suddenly rose in his mind.

"I read a report in the recent edition of Emergency Medicine of people hearing chimes before losing consciousness. It appears to be something of an emergent phenomenon. Haven't we all experienced dreams where we've obtained something great and awoken to find it missing? Just last week I dreamt I had a gold bar in my hand. When I awoke, I was gripping my forearm, which was numb from sleeping on it. But it appears that you're the first person in human history, as far as I'm aware, to have come back from a dream and returned with something substantial. By the way, you wouldn't have stolen that acorn from an arboretum, would you have Mr. Waters? By way of a prank, for instance?"

"No, of course not," Aaron replied, barely following because he was once again daydreaming about food and drink.

"No, of course not. We could have the mineral content analyzed to determine its origins by identifying the geological soil profile and thus its actual grow site. You understand, don't you Aaron? We'll know if you're lying."

"That's fine, I know what I saw," Aaron replied testily, though he suddenly doubted himself because he didn't understand what the doctor was talking about.

He wondered if maybe someone was playing a joke on him. Bulkowitz could've slipped the acorn in his pocket and then Joey gave him that Gummy Nugs© stuff, whatever it was, making him dream all of it up. But it all seemed so real. And he didn't think they could pull off such an elaborate jape.

"Alright, just making sure," the doctor smiled, "we'll keep this acorn for now."

Just then, Ralph Burgman burst into the room.

"We need that acorn, Doc. Aaron, get up. You're not in trouble, but we're going."

"We should keep Mr. Waters here until his condition is fully stable. He's had a rough day, you see?"

The doctor backed up into the corner and tried to put the acorn in his coat pocket on the sly.

"He looks pretty stable to me. Tell him you want your acorn back, Waters."

Aaron began to panic and hit the call button for the nurse by mistake, who had finished her smoke break and came in presently.

"Yes?" she greeted her patient with an odorous tobacco funk.

"I guess we're ready to go, nurse. So, if it's not a problem, could you remove my IV? And Doctor," he said, now addressing Dr. Horn, "I want my acorn back."

"Well, you see... because of the arbitration provision we—

"Unfortunately, Dr. Horn, um... Mr. Waters rejected the arbitration provision upon his arrival," the nurse informed Dr. Horn.

The doctor huffed and tossed the acorn onto Aaron's lap as the nurse worked to free him from his intra-venous tubing. Dr. Eddy Horn brusquely walked past the others, out into the hall, and towards his office mumbling to himself the whole way. He felt frustrated at their unwillingness to cooperate. That, and he didn't know whom to berate. The phenomenon he'd read about in otherwise healthy patients hearing bells and getting taken into a fantasy realm seemed related and yet... *I should've gotten a piece of that acorn to test if only to put my mind at ease.* In any event, he told himself, he would need to correspond with those doctors who had seen similar patients. He then wondered if he should alert the authorities. It was after all still possible that an arboretum was missing an acorn.

The nurse gingerly pressed a small cotton ball on the puncture in Aaron's arm and smiled.

"There, you're all patched up. How are you feeling?"

"Just confused, I guess. They made such a big fuss about me making this stuff up or hallucinating it and now it turns out I might have been right all along. I don't know," he looked at Burgman for support.

"Well, I do," Burgman jumped in. "When we find that Oak, you and I, we'll be sitting pretty. The whole department will know our names."

"Think about it, Waters. From what you told us it's a nice one, too. There will be bids on it from here to China! It will probably break records. And it's on our contracted lot so we get to share in a piece of that action, says so in the Last Gasp laws that still stand to this day!" Burgman bellowed, smacking Aaron on the shoulder with one of his big leathery paws.

"Wow, sounds like you guys stumbled onto something good. I wish I'd get a chance to see an Oak. I've only ever seen a real Tree a couple of times. And I heard you saw a squirrel too? That's crazy. To think that there are still *wild animals* out there," the nurse spoke in such a cadence and with just the right velocity of speech that all the attention in the room went to her and a vacuum of silence ushered in around the others.

"Well, looks like you boys are all set," Dr. Horn told them as he returned from his office, "I guess the front desk already has receipt of your insurance voucher. They just need a signature for the receipt of the voucher receipt along with your license plate number to cover the parking fee. Thanks for coming to see us."

The nurse flashed a smile and Aaron looked at her for the first time since his arrival.

"Here are some electrolyte packs to put in your hydro tanks... sorry you have to get back out there in this heat... some kind of March, huh? We don't usually get like this type of sweltering until June!"

There was something so nurturing about her. The way she emoted with her eyes paired just so with her voice. She sounded so ebullient in the midst of what had turned out to be such a strange day. Aaron needed to know.

" Excuse me, I hope you don't mind me asking your name?" he asked sheepishly.

"It's Gloria. Gloria Day. Happy to make your acquaintance, Mr. Waters!" She smiled again, closing her eyes and letting her chalky teeth sparkle.

The final curse of entanglement was when he shook her hand. His supervisor was looking at them but Aaron didn't care enough at the moment to acknowledge him. He let go of her hand and in what was an uncharacteristically bold move for him, he took one of the electrolyte packets and wrote his name and tracer number on it.

"Now you can contact me if you like," he told her, handing her the packet. *She's kinda making me sick,* he thought. *I feel I could love her.*

The three of them filed out of the room and down the hall, awkwardly splitting at the front desk of the practice.

After the two men had left, Dr. Horn came out of the woodwork and took his nurse's attention as she was walking down the hall past his office.

"Nurse Day, just a moment."

"Yes, Dr. Horn?"

"Gloria, I saw that the patient that just left gave you his tracer information. I need you to get close to that man and learn all you can about him. This may be our chance to finally produce something noteworthy in this place."

"Right, so you want me to just go off and stalk him, or something...?"

"No, you will call him and make plans. And get to know him. Understand?"

"I guess so. Tell me, am I getting overtime for this little mission of yours?" she asked as the doctor walked away.

"We'll see."

At the threshold between the clinic and the outside world, Aaron and Ralph stepped out of two sets of automatic doors into the oppressive heat. They were immediately sweating. Aaron was still feeling adrenaline from his electrolyte-packet tracer-number gambit, but whatever they had given him in the IV seemed to make him immune to the heat for the time being.

CHAPTER 5

Once outside the clinic building and onto the blistering hot asphalt where they could both get signal, Ralph Burgman's tracer lit up with several missed calls and voice messages. It seemed the department was desperate to contact him, so he called regional HQ and Buck D'Aster picked up on the first ring. Ralph thought, *Weird, they usually let it go to voicemail after lunch.*

"Burgman, what the fuck?!" The familiar voice broke through the earpiece.

Ralph and Buck went way back, Ralph had started on Buck's brush crew. Buck was a good guy, but a little gung-ho. He had started his career in the outdoors before Ralph, during the Last Gasp logging effort. Once, after they'd been relegated to fiberweed management, Ralph had seen him solo an entire five-man tract in one 18-hr day just to finish out a contract early enough to get the cash bonus.

"Buck, what's up?"

"Burg, you've got the entire department breathing down my neck about this Tree. What are the coordinates of the Oak, Ralph?"

"I'm not sure, we'll need to check the helm my guy was wearing," Burgman panted back into the microphone.

"Well, make that your priority. We're worried about people hurting themselves because they want to catch a glimpse of a wild squirrel," Buck said with derision.

"Alright Buck, we'll get you those coordinates ASAP," Ralph hung up and took a few big drafts of hot air.

While that conversation went on, Aaron tripped a little on his shoe and smeared himself onto the cracked pavement. Sheer embarrassment forced him to pick himself up quickly and he hid his skinned elbow as he limped subtly back to the truck with his boss.

The three other guys on the crew were lounging in the air-conditioned cab of the idling work truck. It was taking up seven parking spaces with the toter hitched and had racked up three carbon in fees. By the time Aaron Waters and Ralph Burgman returned, Mark Bulkowitz and Joey Dimanche had dozed off, but Pete Barbour was listening to the FM radio.

"News of the Oak sighting has been leaked somehow," Pete said to Burgman as the door to the driver's seat was opened.

"They're saying it's the biggest wild Tree anyone's seen in a decade. Not since the Last Gasp," his voice trailed off as they all tuned in to the sound of a man's voice coming through the speakers.

Welcome back, folks. If you're just joining us, we're following the story of a huge wild Oak Tree spotted somewhere in the thick fiberweed brush of coastal south Florida. A brush crew working for the state's Department of Permaculture stumbled upon the giant log earlier today. They had to evacuate due to a medical emergency, and the exact location isn't currently known. Already people are arguing over what should be done with the relic. Environmental groups are calling for its immediate destruction, saying if it is allowed to reproduce it could create a forest and wipe out the energy-producing fiber barrens that we all depend on for fuel and which the State of Florida derives a good chunk of its revenue. Retired loggers and foresters are saying it should be preserved and allowed to reproduce and multiply so that jobs can be created from the harvest of its offspring. Whatever we each individually think, we must all gaze in wonder at how something so huge could go undetected for so long.

"Yeah, really. Buck and I must've brushed that exact spot 3 times in the past 10 years," Ralph said softly to the radio.

"How could you miss it?" Pete asked earnestly.

"Honestly I don't know. I'll believe it when I see it, acorn or nay-corn," Ralph responded, the good-spirited pun splitting his black beard into a toothy smile.

Aaron turned quiet right about that time. He was deep in thought about that Tree, especially the shade it had provided. *How could he be the only one to experience such a thing? How could it have escaped detection so long?* He continued to ponder these things as the truck pulled out of the emergency clinic parking lot and began the long journey back to the garage.

Everyone that had fallen asleep on the ride jolted awake when Burgman slammed on the breaks as he pulled in to park on the gravel lot to the lock-up where they stored their tools.

"Go home," he told them without anger, "we'll meet at the trailhead tomorrow, not here at the lock-up."

Aaron plopped the acorn from his pocket absent-mindedly into the map compartment of the door to the back seat of the truck and exited the vehicle feeling somehow defeated. This was a normal way for him to feel at the end of the workday but with the skinned elbow on top of a trip to the emergency room and everything else, Aaron felt extra licked.

Ralph Burgman proceeded to log into the helm that Aaron had been using and after a little technical trouble was able to send the coordinates to Buck at his regional workstation. He recognized the area and was certain he'd seen nothing even close to an Oak Tree in that vicinity during the handful of times that he had worked the area. He started to suspect that there was something amiss, but couldn't quite come up with any reasonable explanation, and that irked him. Buck was a guy who liked being prepared for his day, but for tomorrow he felt unprepared, and it was only Wednesday.

Ralph Burgman drove from the garage where he met his work crew every morning to the DoP regional headquarters where he picked up and dropped off paperwork. Swiping his security key, he gave a cool "how-are-ya" to the clerk at the desk. He found Buck in his office with his legs kicked up.

"Burgman! You got those coordinates?" he said, getting his legs off his desk.

"Buck, I don't know man. I've looked at his helm, and you 'n' I hit that section at least twice in the last five years. We would've seen a Tree if it was there," he related to his former partner.

"Yeah, I think it sounds fishy too. No one's seen a wild one in more than a decade. At least not on this continent. And now I hear there's a century Tree out in prime fiber territory? Well, in any case, everyone from the old loggers to Joe Public to the national news and everyone in between has all heard the story by now. So, we better go through the motions anyhow," Buck said tiredly.

"Alright, well I'm going home. See you out there tomorrow?"

"It's going to be another circus. But hey, it's not like it's our first one, right? Remember when we first started thrashing the brush out there, all the protest groups saying we had to let it grow or else the climate would be destroyed? And then they drive home in their DVs burning E85, the very fuel we produce out here!" Buck scoffed.

"There are idiots everywhere," Ralph replied tiredly, trying his best to keep the conversation from going anywhere.

Aaron noticed that traffic was unusually sparse driving back to his apartment. The DVO lane was almost empty: a strange detail to top off a fruity day like the sundae's cherry. His Honda puttered merrily upon the newly paved street in downtown Tampa after navigating the dead highway without incident. Soon he would be at his apartment. His place was a slice of a larger one divided illegally in four by drywall and plaster and a vinyl shower curtain. His room was the one behind the shower curtain. The other residents who shared the floor with Aaron were like strangers to him. They shared a small concrete parking area but used different entrances. He was sure he knew their names but never needed to speak with them. No one was around that night anyhow and he unlocked the door and set foot inside the small single room flat Throwing his keys on the table and his bag on the floor, he went to the fridge and looked inside. There were condiments, half-empty, and some hardened leftovers but nothing edible. He grabbed a can of Miller High Life and retired to the couch. *Could he really have napped in the shade of an Oak today?* He was so very tired; he was weary beyond reckoning, he was soul-tired. Before he could finish his dinner, he had fallen asleep.

It was hours before one of his flatmates came home and loudly shut the front door and the one to her room, the latter behind a deadbolt. Aaron awoke sometime between the two slammed doors and looked around the empty flat. The bare light bulb that lit the flat from the kitchen area in the corner seemed to be losing the battle against the darkness of night. Aaron shut his eyes once more but the distant light wasn't going to let him fall asleep again.

He picked up his tracer to read some headlines from the news feed. Stories drifted slowly up from the ubiquitous technology in his palm, a shoddy hologram now illuminating his corner of the room:

Wild Tree Discovered in Florida Fiber Fields

Jellyfish Harvest Breaks Records

Colonial Expedition to Mars Departure Delayed

Gummy Nugs© Co. Extracts a Big Hit

He swiped at the first story but hit the second one instead and a video began to play in 3D. Hordes of sea-blue jellyfish swam across his tiny area in a crackly, holographic moving picture. The voice of the narration was a simulation he had chosen in his personal network settings. Here and there he found the Imperial British female voice soothing.

"Warmer, more acidic waters are fueling an explosion of jellyfish in the Gulf of Mexico. Researchers at the University of Florida estimate that over 1 trillion jellyfish will be taken in fluthers from the Gulf alone this season. Local fishing fleets out of work from the shrimp decline work with close supervision of the State of Florida and sell their catch to MonDow Corp., who then dry and desalinate smacks of the slimy critters to add nitrogen and minerals back to the soils of their many cornfields."

I bet those jellyfishing rigs smell awful, he thought to himself. I wonder what that wonderful nurse is doing right now?

As if on cue, the illusion of the fluther in his living room was dissolved into indigo sparks and his ringtone played the jingle for an incoming call from an Unknown Caller. He fumbled for the device to answer before it went to his generic voicemail message.

"Hello?" he rasped as he cleared his throat.

"Hello? Is that you, Aaron? Can you hear me?" a female voice responded. It was Gloria.

"Yeah, hi. It's late, what's going on?" Aaron said trying not to sound terse.

"Oh, nothing. I was just watching an article about the Tree you found. I thought I'd give you a call and see how you're doing. Did I wake you? You aren't lying in bed, are you?"

"No, I'm not in bed," he told her.

Technically I'm on a couch, he thought.

"Oh. Well, I just wanted to check in, I guess. I was really glad you gave me your number. I think it's so cool you found a Tree and some squirrels. It's all anyone at the clinic can talk about, especially Dr. Horn. He seems almost jealous!"

"Thanks, I still don't know what to make of it. And it was only one squirrel."

"Oh, but that's still cool. I read that they used to call a group of squirrels a 'scurry.' I bet you didn't know that!" Aaron could feel her smiling through the airwaves. He smiled too.

"No, I didn't. I didn't know they ever grouped up. It's sort of a scary thought. I just learned what jellyfish are called in a group," he offered her.

"A fluther!" she responded instantly. "I love animals. All I ever see are palmetto bugs. And sometimes citrus rats and the crows obviously but they don't really count."

Her charm doesn't translate over the phone, Aaron sensed.

"I'd like to chat some more but it's late and I–"

"Oh no, I didn't mean to bother you, I just was hoping to hear more about it but you must be exhausted, don't let me keep you, really," she assured him.

"It's okay," he said.

There was a moment of silence where neither of them could think of anything else to say. Anxiety was building around the silence. Finally, Aaron had to break out of it.

"Well, I need to get up early for work, I'm sure you understand," he told her.

"Oh, of course. Me too. I bet you guys will be busy with that Tree for a while."

"Yeah. Hey, Gloria?"

"Yes?"

"Do you want to meet up tomorrow after work?" he asked.

"I'd like that. Where should we meet?"

"I don't know yet," he said sleepily.

"Ok, well... have a good night."

"Night."

He could imagine her warm smile through the audio-only connection. It was strange; he felt a tingly restlessness after that conversation. He couldn't stop thinking about her voice and the smile of hers that he could telepathically sense. *What is her deal?* He wondered.

Lacking the will to get up and brush his teeth, he scrunched himself up into a ball and fell back asleep on his couch, ignoring the light. As he closed his eyes, he saw kaleidoscopic patterns on the back of his eyelids, but he didn't give it any serious thought and soon the visions yielded to the void of deep sleep.

When Aaron woke again, it was dark except for the single standard-issue fluoro bulb hanging from a bare wire in the middle of his flat. He pinged his tracer, 4:23 AM. He rolled over and fell back to sleep.

This time his mind was enchanted by a strange personality. In this dream he walked down a dirt road, straight and flat, with this female companion. As he walked down the road, he saw that instead of swathes of familiar fiberweed lining the sides of the road, there were great constructs forming a roof above him. They were columns with arms and fingers that filtered the light of the sun producing a false twilight. Aaron quivered beneath the limbs of these giants. His companion giggled and that eased his worried mind.

<<Our leafy friends are devouring the light>> the bubbly voice relayed joyfully, soundlessly.

She hopped into the air, began to float, and shrank into something else. Something less human, more machine, and whizzed about. She hovered in one place, sort of like that golden fly had before.

So tired of tarrying with the world. My car, my crew, all my money spent for someone else to line their pockets... Aaron thought as he looked at the ground with dread in his dream. In doing so he forgot the towering giants and only saw the road ahead of him.

<<But that's not the light!>> she pleaded with him, immediately and telepathically understanding his negative thought patterns.

He remembered the constructs that lined the boulevard that they were strolling along. *Were they Trees? Centuries-old? Become like cathedrals?* The pillars lined the stage for his companion, this flying little angel-machine shape shifter. He listened to her, completely enraptured.

<<You'll remember the light, won't you? >>

She projected her voice into his mind without speaking, her eyes sparkling like polished stone, her lips holding a thin smile.

The last thing he remembered about the dream was a belly laugh and tears rolling down his face. She was buzzing about, telling him a story with rhymes and puns. He woke up well-rested, but he couldn't remember anything about the story this strange dream being had relayed.

CHAPTER 6

"He gets high on you and the energy you trade,
He gets right on to the friction of the day."

-Rush, *Tom Sawyer*

When Aaron woke up again, the room was filled with natural light. He immediately knew from the angle of the light that he had overslept. Sitting up, he cursed and the weight of the world fell upon his shoulders. Like Atlas, he wondered if he had a choice to go into work or if he could shrug it off. There was no money left, not considering that he had just settled the carbon taxes left over from the winter, plus his rent was about to be due. He also felt pain from hunger. He decided that he had no choice but to drag his sorry ass back to work, or he would surely starve out on the street. It was an unpleasant realization, but worse was remembering his discovery of a rare and ancient Tree the previous day, which seemed somehow less real than the fantastic dream from which he'd just awoken. Aaron couldn't guess the meaning of any of these things – the Tree, the dream, his slobbishness, or his poverty. On his way to the sink, he stubbed his left pinky toe and got pretty mad. His anger reminded him of the anger he felt when he was released from the regional housing camp when he had turned 18 and was no longer a ward of the State. He still felt the frustration of being so unprepared for the harsher reality of life on the outside.

He'd only owned it for almost two years, but his Honda Squire was 20 years-old and still ran pretty reliably. There was perhaps no other day of that vehicle's life when a man's job depended on it more, but who knows? Though Aaron only had to fix it once in the last year and a half, he greatly respected that vehicle for its longevity. Aside from that one fix it had done its job without much complaint. Aaron would now have to draw on his rapport with this machine, for this morning he knew he would have to push his luck at every intersection to have a chance to make it to work even remotely on time. More late than normal, perhaps he could make up the time in a series of gambles on the highway...

The highway was not at all backed up for a change. Maybe it was the time of morning, being slightly later than his usual commute. The traffic pattern was flowing at or above the speed limit when he merged. He immediately got over into the passing lane, and although he wasn't going as fast as the few cars in the DVO lane, he was at least passing the rest of the vehicles on the road. He looked down at the dash.

Fuel: enough.

Engine temp: straight up the middle.

No weird lights on the dashboard at all.

He pressed the accelerator with his big toe. It looked like he might not be late if the traffic kept up like this. Lacking any breakfast, he felt hungry and began to sweat. Knowing there were breakfast bars on the floor of the passenger side he reached smartly and felt for one. *Aha!* His fingers felt one rectangular prism of cornmeal and insect protein sealed in a plastic wrapper. Stubbornly it tumbled through his hands and into the crack between the seat and the center console. Again he reached and felt, but this time came up empty like his stomach. He looked down and saw it, right where he was reaching as if he had reached straight through a hologram.

Aaron reached once more and squeezed the food bar, focusing on it now. One hand on the wheel, the other attempting to unwrap the food shape, he dizzily concentrated in a delicate operation of navigation and procurement. The jingle of a bell between his ears triggered him to push the clutch pedal, cutting power to the transmission, and in his peripheral vision, he noticed something unlikely: a great body of metal drifting from the DVO lane towards his vehicle.

He jammed his foot down on the brake, but the rusted-out line couldn't handle the force and snapped under the strain. At the same time, his other foot slipped off the clutch. The twenty-year-old Honda jerked and bucked as the transmission struggled. In his rearview he could see the cars behind him swerved into the middle lane to avoid the obvious mess and get around the impending collision, and by doing so blocked his only exit to his side. The intruding vehicle had bounced over the DVO buffer zone and into his lane, squishing his left side-view mirror and pushing him out into the passing traffic, which was desperately trying to worm its way around the ugly two-car snarl.

Horns blared around them as the two vehicles courted. Aaron turned the wheel into the invading vehicle's direction to keep the two of them from being sideswiped by a tractor-trailer bearing down his passenger's side. The Squire had little more than a thin layer of steel between him and the cars now rocketing past him on the right. The two vehicles, now enmeshed, came to a grinding halt in the white-striped DVO lane buffer. When he came to a stop, Aaron found that his door was jammed shut so he scrambled to crawl out the passenger side of his tin can. It now seemed clear to him that he absolutely would not be making it to work on time.

The other driver still had not exited their vehicle by the time Aaron had positioned himself in a safer location. Horns sounded around the crash but in fewer numbers as he tried to get the driver's attention. He felt awkward but he made brief eye contact after waving and was reasonably assured that they were well enough and didn't intend him any harm. He approached their driver side door and the single occupant seemed to be on the phone and looking purposefully away. He brought himself to tap on the tinted glass window. No response. He knocked and waited and knocked again.

"Okay, I see you. What?" she snipped at him, lowering the window a crack.

"Well, you hit me and I –"

"I DID NOT hit you! My damn car went bonkers and I couldn't even control it manually!" she huffed at him from behind the window.

Aaron didn't know how to respond. She was obviously delusional. Her new eggnog-colored autopilot BMW was hardly even scratched after it had entirely wrecked his Honda.

"I don't know how to ..." Aaron pleaded, grasping for words.

"I don't know what you want from me. I'm trying to get my insurance company on the phone but I'm only getting recordings," she offered meekly.

Her beady brown eyes pierced the window and looked for his response, and her shiny, even bangs shielded her fear-creased forehead. Her pale white skin gleamed from behind the tint of the window. Aaron felt his own brown complexion flush with anger.

"Well, my brakes went out in the collision and I'm late to work and just thought maybe we could carpool," Aaron reasoned with her.

He was hoping she wouldn't see his masked frustration and instead agree to this proposal especially since he didn't have insurance.

"Hold on, let me call my lawyer," she told him and rolled up the window.

Cars continued to honk going by, mostly from those in the piloted vehicle lanes. In the DVO lane, Aaron noticed the piloted vehicles were taking the field, evidently taking advantage of the space offered up from the missing driverless cars. He wondered why there were so very few DVs on the road. Whatever it was, perhaps it had caused this wreck too. He looked around and sighed. The highway exhaust fumes and dust stung his eyes. It was getting hot. The wind from cars going by in the DVO lane blew the fiberweed over in the central highway divider. A diesel tractor-trailer honked and snapped him from daydream into anxiety. He was still sweating. It was then he realized he had forgotten to put on deodorant and tried to block out his embarrassment.

"Hey, my lawyer said you can get in the car with me as long as I take a picture of your license and send it to him."

Aaron reached for his wallet and walked to her door. She took his license and snapped a picture with her tracer.

"Hey! You're that guy that discovered the wild Tree. I saw your name come up on my tracer last night. All right, you can jump in the back. Just move the stuff," she said, unlocking the doors and gesturing to a small briefcase, some clothes, and some trash on the floor."

"I'm Aaron, what's your name?" he asked, piling into the new vehicle and swamping out a space for him.

"It's Angelena, but everyone calls me Lena."

"Ok, thanks for letting me in Lena. It's pretty scary out there."

"My God, I know. I can't believe they let the newest virus in from Asia. It's terrible," she said, looking down at her scrolling news feed.

Aaron was referring to the heat and the traffic. He didn't know what she meant about the Asian virus. Was it a software bug or a biological one? He decided he wouldn't press the issue, now that he was safe inside her vehicle. He could look it up later. Her car smelled so clean. No fumes, just fresh junk food trash and that new car smell he had heard about in advertisements.

"So, what happened? I heard the new DVs were giving people trouble, but that was crazy!" he asked, trying to quell a growing silence.

"Oh yeah, that? I have no idea. It was so stupid, my car just stopped playing my Storytime and I looked up and I was drifting out of the lane, and it wouldn't take my commands! I was like: 'get back in our lane! ACK!!'" She gestured wildly in an odd outburst and looked back at Aaron who was now in utter disbelief at the absurdity of the person who had been thrown into his lap.

"Anyway, I have to get to work or I'll lose out on the morning Dunkin' order. My lawyer said I should just take you in and ask the company for a loaner car," she told him regretfully, pressing her fingerprint into the ignition button to start the engine.

"Do you think my car will be alright there? What about your car, is it all right now?

"Oh, I'm sure it has some terrible scratches and some paint missing. But it should be fine. These things are built to withstand impact from a meteor," she nonchalantly informed him.

Aaron didn't see how that could be possible, but he didn't say anything.

A tracer commercial popped into his mind of a meteor hitting a car and the lady opening her car door and walking away unscathed. She didn't even have to get out of the passenger side like Aaron just did. He thought Lena saw (and misunderstood) the same ad, and that she literally believed that her car was meteor-proof.

"I guess my car will have to wait. Hopefully, they will just impound it. Hell, it must be totaled. What do I care, right?" Aaron asked her.

Lena ignored him and continued to monitor her tracer feed as the vehicle pulled itself away from the scene of the wreck.

"Engage Navigation: work," she said to her vehicle.

Navigation engaged. Now en route to MonDow Corp. regional administration building.

"Engage Storytime: *Princess and Her Horse Ride to a Villa,*" she commanded as the vehicle began to pick up speed.

Storytime engaged. Now playing *Incest Murder-Horse of Valhalla.*

"Wait, what??" Lena asked of the aloof female-voiced automobile computer.

"Sleipnir? Sleipnir!! HEY SLIPPY!!!" Odin cracked a huge thunderbolt and called again for his 8-legged steed who was carrying his deadly weapons.

"Wait, leave it on. This sounds pretty cool," Aaron squeaked from the back, barely above the now-booming voice of the computer.

"SLIPPY COME ON. Bring me my Gungnir. We ride for Hel."

"What the fuck? Disengage Storytime! Damn it!!" Lena cried and hit the dashboard of the speeding vehicle.

"At least it's staying in the lines now. That was the right destination though, right?" Aaron spoke coolly from the back seat.

"No, we're going to WORK, not HELL!" She puffed back at him.

Storytime disengaged. Now driving to Worknot Hill.

Aaron could barely contain an outburst of laughter. He was silently grateful to be in an air-conditioned vehicle for one of the only times of his entire life. The computer had obliged to end the tale of the thunder god and his leggy horse, which he was only a little disappointed about. *But hey: easy come, easy go.* They were moving at least, and staying in the DVO lane, which was all but completely forsaken by other traffic. This last fact was slowly starting to disturb him, but he decided to make no fuss. He was just along for the ride.

"Engage: Radio. Station: News traffic tidbits," Lena dictated to the automobile.

Radio engaged. You are now listening to News, Traffic, and Tidbits.

just don't know if they'll ever be seen again. That's the gambit, it's all or nothing. If they're able to set up their colony dome then certainly we'll be hearing from them but in transit, they will—

"Oh, this must be the Mars pilgrims setting off! What are their names again?" Aaron asked the automobile and Lena.

"Who cares? There's a trillion-carbon deficit and we're sending people to Mars? It's so irresponsible," the lady responded, quoting her counterpoint afternoon news hour.

have their location and trajectory mapped out, but the only information we'll have about them, themselves, is their vitals and the fact that their preservation chambers are functioning. And this journey, folks, is brought to you by the refreshing taste of classic Coca-Cola. Mmm … Crisp and Delicious! And, by MonDow lawn tamer. It's not just your lawn; it's your life!

"Have you tried the new Coke flavor experience? I want to like it but sometimes I just don't know. I'll try it again after lunch and see what I think," Lena asked as she flashed a glancing pair of probing eyes at him through the rear-view mirror.

"No, I don't do virtual reality. But my coworker brought in this weird vaporizer ... Gummy Nugs? It was nice. Tasted like, fruity, and just lovely," Aaron told her, using a tone and words that were out of character for him, especially in the company of a stranger. He blushed in the back seat.

"Oh my god, I love the Dunkin coffee vaporizers. I think the French vanilla salt roast is my favorite," Lena confided in him.

"So, you work for MonDow? I actually work cutting fiberweed. What's MonDow like?" Aaron asked, feeling open now.

"It's pretty chill," she told him.

The rest of the drive was uneventful. Aaron felt comfortable sitting in silence now that they had bonded over having both vaporized things. And they were both relieved that Lena's vehicle's computer had no more surprises in store for them. They made it to MonDow's regional administrative building where Aaron was able to get a good look at Lena for the first time on the walk through the sweltering parking lot. Her skin-tight suit was designed to wick heat and moisture off her body and make her look professional at the same time. She was still young but showing signs of aging. She was not very muscular, not like Gloria. Gloria was used to working with her hands, helping people. Lena was used to being helped, by other people and by machines, which the folds of flesh and fabric in her back illustrated.

They walked into the huge, air-conditioned mono-lith that was the MonDow regional HQ, and Lena swiped Aaron in as a guest. She seemed relieved to be in the cooler atmosphere and she was breathing quickly from the physical exertion of leaving her vehicle. The lobby of the MonDow regional administration building was filled with negative space and indoor plants. There were a dozen or so empty lounge chairs and lonely cafe tables littered in front of large windows. A single receptionist guarded the computer at the desk before the elevator. They walked past the person without making any contact. Lena's swipe at the door had sufficed.

"We just need to ride the elevator to the fifth floor and then we can sit and relax for a bit. And we can put in our order for Dunkin. I usually get a fizzy-iced coffee swirl, mocha index 3, and a breakfast bomb," Lena said in stride, half to Aaron and half to herself.

"Great! And then maybe we can see about getting a car for me?"

"Yeah, definitely. That shouldn't even be a problem. There's like 20 company vehicles out back."

The fifth floor was an aesthetically dead war zone over-flowing with trashcans, coffee rings, and cubicles. The pot-ted plants in the corners by the windows were covered with layers of dust, and appeared more gray than green after years of sunlight faded the green plastic. That was where a cou-ple of nervous interns were pacing, about to take the daily Dunkin order. The fluorescent lights and the carpet, hard-ened with age, made Aaron feel confined in a cage, like a prisoner or an animal. But at least it was nice and cool. He was even starting to feel a chill.

"Let's get our order in, quick. What do you want?" Lena asked him with a sudden urgency.

"Just coffee and a bagel."

"What kind?"

"Huh?"

"What kind of coffee and what kind of bagel?" she asked impatiently.

"Regular... normal, with nothing," he replied, hoping this was something that they served.

"Um, okay," she frigidly wrote their orders on the clip-board at the front of the vast room and gestured Aaron to follow her back.

Aaron never got to eat out. His budget for food was also his budget for beer and fuel. He wasn't good at budgeting because he didn't have enough money to make a budget.

They made their way through the labyrinth of cubicles. Overhearing the chatter of the workplace he became grateful he didn't work in a place like that. *All these people,* he thought. *Every day, back and forth. What do they come here for? What are they **doing**?*

"Did you see that one with the human driver who got LOST? Ohmygawd I could've died laughing," someone said from behind a cubicle wall.

"It wasn't until the end that you figure out that her house had toxic gas in it and she was the crazy one the whole time," came a voice from a different cubicle interface.

"...mission to *Mars*! Colonists! We can't even keep our driverless vehicles from going completely bonkers and now we're sending people on a terminal mission? This country has got its priorities completely –"

My god, Aaron thought, *they're all just talking about the article vids on their tracers. They aren't doing any actual work at all. This must be what they do every day. They're like living radio transmitters. Taking in messages and positions and opinions and then relaying them out to other receivers.*

"So, what do you do here?" Aaron asked his new companion earnestly.

"My job title is Digital Media Assistant. I make us look good and reply to idiots straight to their tracers," she smiled sardonically.

"Oh, neat," Aaron lied.

He followed her to her cubicle, where she booted up her computer. "Everything in order," she cracked a slight smirk and sighed.

"Alright, let's go talk to Jerry and see if he can't get you a loaner car," she relented to Aaron, whom she could sense was beginning to feel like a captive in her presence.

They walked to the only office with an actual door, all the way across the floor again. Nondescript music in a foreign tongue registered throughout the airwaves. Aaron couldn't tell if it was an intercom or someone's radio. It made it impossible to hear more or less than two conversations at once.

"Her cat was just so sick she couldn't do anything but..."

"... and that's when the car just slowed down to a complete stop in the middle of the DVO lane. I could've died right then and there!"

"... the Dunkin order better arrive soon because I am *literally* **dying** here. I almost fell asleep in the middle of a conference call."

"That wouldn't be the first time."

These people just have no idea how lucky they are to be in an air-conditioned building all day. And yet... I could never. They're all so dull. Replicas of each other. Stories already told. On and on. Like a mirror to a mirror. Back and forth forever. Not for any amount of carbon would I...

Aaron felt his mind dying of cynicism by the time they reached Jerry's office. He wondered how late he could be to his own job and still keep it. Especially today, when everyone would want to ask him questions. He was a shadow in the spotlight, but for how long? At some point, he'd get a car and have to go into the brush, find his crew and face reality. There would be a huge Tree there or there wouldn't.

What if there wasn't?

He would probably lose his job if they couldn't find the Oak. But then, he probably wouldn't even get to work until lunch and he'd be fired for that, too. He imagined himself walking up and the crew was eating lunch. If they had found the Oak, they would be cracking jokes and celebrating their fortune. 'Who cares if Aaron's late again? He's always late!' But then if the Oak Tree wasn't found they'd be pissed off. 'Why are we out here looking for your stupid Tree when we have a contract to finish?' they'd say, and he'd be canned for being late.

"Hey! Pay attention now. Let me do the talking," Lena growled at him.

Aaron nodded his assent and watched as Lena put her smile on and opened the door to Jerry's office without knocking.

"Hi, Jerry! Good morning! You're looking sharp," she beamed at the slim, pale man behind a large messy desk with fake wooden veneer.

The sharp odor of morning breath hit Aaron in the face. It smelled like someone had slept there last night.

Is there any ventilation in here at all? Aaron wondered.

"Good morning, Angelena. And who is your friend here?" the man inquired listlessly, looking up from his tracer through thick, circular spectacles.

Aaron noticed that his suit was faded. The lines in the man's face revealed that he had been tired for a very long time. *How could a man who supervises people who don't seem to work much look so very tired? He must bank a ton of carbon ... why wouldn't he get a nicer suit? Doesn't he care?*

Then Aaron looked down at his own worn denim work pants. *Perhaps the man thinks the same of me.*

"This is ... hey what's your name again? He's the guy who found the Oak Tree!" Lena cheerfully introduced him.

"It's Aaron. Waters," he said, trying to decide if he should reach in and shake hands with the man seated at the tacky office desk.

"I see. Interesting," Jerry responded.

A moment went by with Jerry stroking his stubbly chin as if deep in thought. Lena did an uncomfortable little shuffle as Aaron observed them both. Jerry seemed half here; half somewhere else. His gray unkempt hair and gray suit and the morning breath and the glassy eyes seemed to slow the passage of time.

"So, I was wondering if we could get a loaner car for him? Because I … his car broke down and I … picked him up. My lawyer said it would be OK," Lena spoke, breaking the spell of morning silence with a lie or two.

"You picked him up and he wants a car, hmm...?" Jerry seemed to seriously consider her story while also clearly not caring at all.

Aaron realized how ridiculous her story sounded and began to think he wouldn't be getting to work at all today.

"I gotta get to work. Is there a bus or something else I could take? I don't have the money for a Google car or I'd have hired one at the crash."

"Crash? Hmm..." the man again receded into thought.

The two of them stood there for a moment, looked at one another, as Aaron started for the door.

"Wait a minute. I'll send a message to the chief!" Jerry exclaimed, overcoming his mental inertia.

"No, please, you don't have to do that," Lena pleaded.

Jerry disregarded her and began to type at his computer and then hit the 'enter' button with a flourish.

"There!" he said to the universe in general.

CHAPTER 7

"Time to make the donuts."

—Fred the Baker

A knock came from the door before it opened. A pearly-white plump lady with curly blonde hair and a pink power suit announced:

"I'm BA–aacckk!

And Aaron could sense that outside the office a palpable energy wave was initiated throughout the entire floor. The woman in pink placed a brown paper bag and styrofoam beverage container on Jerry's desk.

"Hey, Jerry! Here's your bagel with glitter and your iced honey tea with espresso flavor," she said with enthusiasm.

She left the room and was accosted by 3 or 4 people and more were on the way. She had their fix: bags of breakfast food and special drink orders.

This is perhaps her only function here, Aaron thought. *She takes the Dunkin order and delivers it. And then she makes rounds chatting and socializing. What a gig: it's good work if you can get it.*

"Freedom should be here soon," Jerry said after washing a bite of glitter bagel down with his icy, coffee-flavored drink.

Freedom? Aaron thought. *Here soon?*

"Freedom?" he couldn't help but say it out loud.

"Freedom is the executive vice president of the Company. She's in town and … she's a force," Lena told him.

"A force of nature, that woman," Jerry agreed and took another draft of his iced beverage.

Lena and Aaron stood there while Jerry ate his breakfast and drank his "coffee." There was only one chair in the room and it was directly facing Jerry so it wouldn't have made sense for any one of them to sit down and leave the other standing. Jerry sat admiring his bagel, and then he consumed it with relish, ignoring his two visitors. Because of this he now had glittery cream cheese in his stubble. Aaron could not bear to witness him a moment longer, nor could he look away. He was stuck in time, watching Jerry eat a bagel over and over again.

Soon a knock came to the cracked-open door and a tall blonde woman entered. Her skin was fair and light, her eyes almond-brown. *Or were they green?* She wore cotton candy pink lip-gloss and had French manicured nails, silvery makeup, and bejeweled high heels. An aura of a subtle fragrance seemed to transform even the lighting of the room. This was, as Aaron suspected, Freedom.

"Hey everyone: I can't believe how long the Dunkin order took, right?" she greeted the captive audience in the dingy office, commanding an enthusiastic response to her presence.

"Aaron Waters, enviro tech for Department of Permaculture," Aaron said automatically, extending his right hand as energetically as he could.

"Freedom Vinolte, enchanted to meet you," she told him, shaking his hand amicably. "We're thrilled to have you here. So, Jerry tells me you need a car? I think we can arrange that. We've got a whole fleet out back."

"Jerry, print the release form so we can get Mr. Waters to where he needs to be," she ordered.

"Yes, of course," he registered.

"You can go back to your station unless there is anything else, Miss Biddle," Freedom said, flashing a toothy smile to Lena.

"OK. Thanks for doing this, I'm sorry I—"

"It's not a problem." Freedom cut her off and smirked her out the door.

Freedom took the release form, still warm from Jerry's printer, and put it on the desk in front of Aaron.

"Just fill this out and we can get you a car. I don't know why Jerry couldn't have just handled this," she said, looking disappointedly towards Jerry.

"Freedom, this here is the brusher operator from Permaculture who found that Oak Tree," Jerry finally told her.

Aaron wondered why any of that was relevant here. He could feel Freedom's eyes fix on him now as he filled out the form. It was a simple contract releasing liability and ensuring safe return of property, subject to fines and imprisonment, etc.

"That was *you*? Why didn't you tell me earlier, Jerry!? This is huge!" She voiced, slamming the door thunder-shut and making everyone on the floor's head turn toward the office.

Aaron still didn't see the point of this.

"Yeah, I found it. No one believes me though," he told them, looking up briefly from the form.

"Well, we're livid about it! Right, Jerry?"

Jerry nodded quickly, reflexively agreeing with her.

"We just took a metric ton of fiber rootstock samples out of the very area you made your little discovery. Do you realize we're sponsoring the Mars mission? Do you have any *idea* what this means to us at all?"

Aaron shook his head 'no.'

"We sell tons and tons of growth inhibitor for that shit every year. It grows in the sun, not in the shade of giant fiber-resistant oak trees. No one likes fiberweed around more than your department and us, the people making and selling the crap that beats it back down to a manageable size for lawns. Why do you think we're trying to grow it on Mars?"

"I didn't know … I don't know. Why?" Aaron asked, dumbstruck.

"If we picked up resistant acorns in that sample of rootstock and we start an oak tree on the first colony on Mars, it could completely *fuck up* our business model. And I've got this stupid radio interview in 40 minutes and no one has prepared me any talking points at all whatsoever. We've got how-many-dozens of interns on this floor, all suckling Dunkin from the Company teat, and I have nothing to show for it," Freedom disclosed and backed away from the desk.

Why is she telling me this? Aaron thought to himself. *It seems like she's giving away more than she intended to. I still don't know why they'd want it to grow on Mars.*

"Well, I don't think any Tree could out-compete the fiberweed which grows 10 feet in a season!" Aaron reasoned.

"Yeah, *here* it does that, for now anyway. But on Mars? We'd be lucky to get anything to grow on that God-forsaken hellhole," Jerry interjected.

"Yeah, good luck, right?" Aaron replied earnestly and submitted the signed form to Jerry.

"Jerry, go show him how to get a car," Freedom ordered, wilting against the wall.

Jerry got up obediently, taking his coffee drink with him. It wasn't often he got the chance to leave his office.

The two men left the office wordlessly and headed for the elevator. There was a low hush about the floor. Aaron could tell that people were paying attention to the highly unusual hubbub of Jerry's normally sleepy office, and murmuring about them as they made their way.

"So, Jerry... you got any kids?" Aaron said, trying to thaw the ice.

"Yep, two daughters, both grown up now. One's a software developer in Boston and one's a biophysicist, she's been selected to go on that Mars mission. She's here in Florida right now getting ready. She and her husband are scheduled to go. You may have heard of him. Dr. Raphael Pernici is his name. He's the project's lead astro-medical engineer or something," he said with pride.

I'm sorry I asked, Aaron felt like saying.

"That's great, you must be proud," Aaron said instead.

I wonder if MonDow has anything to do with Jerry's daughter getting assigned to the Mars mission? He wondered, but it didn't bother him too much. Aaron was more concerned with getting a ride to the work site ASAP.

"Of course! She's making history. I just wish there wasn't this mess with the acorns and stuff. Freedom told me some of her higher-ups want to cancel. Said it would be bad for PR and marketing if we grow a forest out there by mistake in those... bio bubbles."

Aaron knew what he was talking about: the great colony domes. They had been testing them for years in the Sahara, and in Death Valley. Now it was looking like the USA would be the first country to have a citizen born on a foreign planet.

"So why are you trying to grow the fiberweed on Mars? Why not corn, or potatoes? Aaron asked, not sure if the answer was proprietary or not.

"I really couldn't tell you. I mean, I don't know. I'm sure Freedom knows," Jerry responded.

As they made their way to the elevator, the door opened. A man and a woman dressed in matching space-jumpers began to exit. Jerry stopped at once.

"Jennifer? I thought you were in Cape Canaveral!" Jerry said, going in for a hug.

"Daddy! They want to cancel our mission!" the woman with misty eyes told her father.

"I was just telling Aaron here that you were in Florida and now here you are! Isn't that fun?" Jerry too began to glisten at the eyes.

"Where's Freedom?" the man accompanying Jennifer asked shortly.

"She's back in Jerry's office I think," Aaron relayed.

Wordlessly the man walked back in that direction. It was immediately clear that Jerry and his son-in-law were not very close and perhaps not even very well acquainted. Aaron suspected that Jerry didn't get a chance to see his daughter very often. *How sad,* he thought, *that he has to run into her at work. Although, he seems to like it here. Maybe it's more home than office to him.*

"We're going out back to get this guy a car, but I'll be right back. Will you be here?" Jerry asked his daughter.

"Yes, Dad. I think so... But I think we're flying out later today. We just ... needed to get something from Freedom in person," the young woman said with hesitation.

A soundless flash of dull white light came from the direction of Freedom's office. *That looked just like a muffled laser pistol in the movies,* Aaron thought. A moment passed. Nothing seemed to change in the office as Dr. Pernici calmly walked towards them.

"Come on honey, let's not keep them. It was great to see you, sir, as always," Dr. Raphael Pernici said to his wife and father-in-law, respectively.

Aaron noticed that Pernici looked clammy and rushed. They continued past Aaron and Jerry.

"Well, I'll see you guys soon, right? I mean, we're just going out back. It shouldn't take but 10 minutes," Jerry seemed to whimper.

The married couple exchanged glances. Raphael Pernici began to walk away faster.

"We're just here for business, Dad. We'll catch up soon though, okay? Maybe I can call you from space later in the week," Jennifer Pernici promised her father over her shoulder.

"It was sure good to see you, Jen. It's been so long! Good luck with the baby, I —" Jerry's appeal was interrupted and his gesture to his daughter's baby bump went unnoticed.

"Let's go, honey," Dr. Pernici cut in.

"Bye, Daddy!"

The Pernicis took off down the stairs and didn't look back.

"They don't *look* like astronauts. Or I guess what I thought astronauts might look like. They just looked like ...", Aaron started to say they looked like pale nerds who would have never seen a hard day's work, then he remembered this was Jerry's family he was talking about.

"I know, but they've been both in school for years and years. I'm into the millions of carbon of debt for her. But it is all going to be worth it when they start a family on Mars. I just can't believe it's really happening!" Jerry said with a twinkle in his eye.

Wow, millions in carbon. What could I do with that? I can't even imagine. New house, nice boat, an auto-drive truck with climate control. What else is there? But maybe that's why Jerry sleeps here: all out of money, nowhere to go, and nothing to do but to keep grinding away at work. I wonder what his daughter would be doing if he hadn't paid for her education.

Inside, the elevator whirred to a nauseating halt. The elevator shaft was revoltingly hot and musty with ageless dust and tropical moisture. The two men exited the elevator onto the ground floor.

Temporary nostalgia bored into Aaron's head with the familiar vision of plants and empty cafe tables. The bottom floor was exactly as it had been before: no more, no less. They made their way past the receptionist and beyond her this time. She looked up and recognized Jerry.

"Jerry! It's nice to see you down here," the receptionist smiled. Her makeup deflected any further scrutiny. The monitor in front of her, the radio to her left, and the tracer to her right all seemed to buttress her in place. She was personally and professionally linked into the grid. The smile she gave informed them they could continue through the lobby. Aaron wondered if she was an android.

"Everyone knows me here," Jerry confided in Aaron.

"Yeah, I can see that," Aaron responded, feeling immediately depressed.

They walked farther along to a gate where Jerry swiped his keycard. Then they walked out of the doors into the blinding midday sunshine and a humidity that could drown a swamp rat.

"Somehow, someday, I'd like to just get away. Go somewhere and do something that no one's ever going to even understand," Jerry said, a man who to Aaron seemed to have lived an entirely predictable life so far.

"I know what you mean," Aaron said, "I can't stand to see those same guys on my crew over and over each week. And never having anything to show for it in carbons."

"Debt aside, I've earned enough carbon but it's turned me into something else. Now I'm just another sucker on the vine. But at least Jennifer is going to make something of her life. Can you imagine? The first woman to land on another planet *and* the first one to give birth in space! I'm so proud. She's the one that makes this all worthwhile. She's going to give birth to the first Martian American. Gosh!" Jerry beamed, wiping a tear and the sweat from under his glasses.

"Do you think you'll be able to visit your grandkids on Mars someday?" Aaron asked Jerry.

"Probably. Heck, I'll probably move there once they've got the support systems up and running. If I can ever retire, that is," Jerry added wistfully.

The fleet of newish vehicles sat in the glaring light and heat of the sun, baking in the brilliance. Heat waves radiated visibly off the cars. The two of them stood there, Aaron and Jerry, wholly strangers and yet bound together by a twist of fate brought on by coincidence. Aaron felt a distant closeness to Jerry. He could understand this man and his lonesome, isolated existence. He too had often wished for something more. But unlike Jerry, he had no one to be proud of and nothing really to look forward to.

"Well, here we are. Take your pick, chief!" Jerry said remotely and handed him a master key.

Aaron was suddenly leaden with dread. His realization was like a physical weight: that soon he would be on his way to his job, late again, *really* late this time, like, the *latest ever*, and on such an important day. *But*, he thought, *a freight train was rolling along and that train was Fate.* He didn't know how or what it was, but somehow Aaron Waters felt an unyielding inertia pulling him onward in spite of, or perhaps because of, his massive psychological unpreparedness for novelty. He would have to choose one of these cars and it would drive him to meet his crew. The more he resisted the pull of the decision to choose a car, the more immediately he would have to make it, and the train kept on driving.

He ended up choosing one close to the razor-wired chain-link fence that surrounded the lot. Fiberweed pushed up, over, and through the fence, nearly engulfing the cars in that row. Aaron reasoned it might be a little bit cooler than the others. It was an uninformed decision, one based on his irrelevant experience of searching for shady parking spaces to leave his ancient Honda Squire. What he didn't understand was that as soon as the key entered the door and unlocked the car it also turned on the engine and the climate control. And the reason the vehicle he chose was close to the fence was because no one used it anymore: it was last year's model. He was unaware of this though and sometimes it turns out that ignorance is bliss.

Aaron jammed the key into the keyhole. At once the windows cracked and hot air blasted out as cool air filled the cabin, all before he could even remove the key from the slot. He looked around at the other cars in the lot and realized he had no way of knowing if any of them was better than any other.

Aaron took a seat in the cab of the automobile and immediately felt naked with no steering wheel, no brakes, no accelerator, no levers or buttons of any kind. *Just a screen?*

"Enjoy the ride, sport. My tracer is listed on the console. Just buzz me when you're done and we'll get you signed out and cleared of liability," Jerry told the bewildered young man who was too overwhelmed to register that information.

In Aaron's mind, Jerry had been transformed from a feckless old hack into the pinnacle of sagacity with that one sentence: *Enjoy the ride, sport.* It became apparent that he knew things about the world that until this point Aaron could only have guessed.

Here was his first ride as the "pilot" of a driverless vehicle. The train was accelerating, and it seemed *no one* was driving.

CHAPTER 8

"Welcome," the interior of the driverless car said to Aaron. The car's atmosphere was pleasant and fresh and presented none of the humidity, heat, or smog from the outside. He watched Jerry walk back into the MonDow regional HQ building and waited for the car to take him to work. But the car wouldn't move.

"Engage," Aaron took a swing.

"User is Engaged. Welcome!" the car responded.

"Engage: Navigation," he tried again.

"Negative, user is not secured," the car came back.

Not secured? Aaron thought. *Seat belt?*

"Engage: Seat Belt," he told the car.

"Seat Belt engaging," the car echoed.

A strap shot out of the frame of the car, almost hitting him in the face. It firmly connected him to the seat. It was incredibly tight, so he pulled on it in an attempt to loosen its grip. The seat belt yielded temporarily but as soon as he let go, the belt fashioned itself even tighter around his waist and along his throat. He struggled a little and the belt chafed against the skin of his neck. Wearing a brush helm and armor was more comfortable.

"Engage: Navigation," he squeaked.

"Navigation. Where are we going?" the car asked.

Shoot, where are we going? Where were we yesterday? The six road, but which marker though?

"Just off 75: the six road, towards Pebble Creek," Aaron replied.

"The six road. North or south?"

"North," Aaron guessed serendipitously.

"Navigation engaged and route calculated. Now driving," the car told him.

The driverless vehicle began to roll out of the gravel lot towards the automated parking booth. The booth's magnetic sensor read the sticker on the windshield and disarmed the tire spikes guarding the gate. The car rolled through it and again Aaron worried about an unstoppable fate train, some invisible cosmic superstructure that was carrying him through space and time.

"Engage, Radio," he ordered, lashing out in an effort to manipulate his slipping grasp on reality.

"Radio, On!" the car answered seemingly with attitude, and a deafening white noise emitted wildly loud throughout the car's interior.

The car was turning out of the MonDow compound and onto a public road and blasting radio static into Aaron Waters' ears from every angle. He looked at the display screen, which read: PLEASE ENTER PROGRAM, STATION OR CHANNEL.

"The News," Aaron guessed.

The voice of the car's computer rose above the white noise and cried:

"You may listen to the News on a multitude of different channels. If you don't specify, a combined approximation will be achieved and presented with a 23-second delay. Please wait."

Twenty-three glorious seconds of silence ensued, and Aaron observed his surroundings fly past like a whisper from the cockpit of the driverless loaner-car. The widened windshield allowed him to see in almost a whole 180-degree view. He fiddled around for a bit but forced himself to relax once he realized he wouldn't need to pay attention or navigate the automobile.

"Welcome to Approximated Radio News Online, 'ARNO.' The developing stories include a dog whose mind has been transferred into a computer and back again. The dog, named Mort, had all of his neural signatures removed and written onto gelatin impregnated with carbon nanotube networks. The network known as Mort was then able to respond to voice commands in the same way Mort the dog earlier demonstrated. When the nanotube network identified as Mort was uploaded again into the organic vessel that had produced Mort in the first place, there was a similar demonstration of command recognition. The dog will have to recover for some time before conclusive indications can be gathered as to the extent of any permanent damage to Mort: the good boy who became a computer then became a dog again."

"Transhumanist groups have called this experiment a 'huge leap of progress,' while others are calling it a blatant ethics violation, inhumane, and claims of animal cruelty may yet be heard in court," ARNO the androgynous voice approximation of the average news caster related to Aaron Waters.

He thought about that dog. *What's it like to be a dog, then a gelatinous carbon-fiber network, and then be a dog again? How do*

I know I'm not some thought pattern downloaded onto a computer, running out a simulation? Electronic dog food must be much less expensive.

Aaron looked out as a few people driving their cars were left behind him while he effortlessly maintained velocity in the DVO lane. The cars in front of him and behind him were empty.

It had taken Aaron a long time to get used to the empty cars. He still couldn't understand why there would be cars driving around with no one inside. It made sense that some-one would send their car out to pick up the groceries, and there were also great fleets of driverless cars giving rides to people or idling in parking lots waiting for them to shop. It seemed to him that at *least* half the time these taxis should have passengers. There must be people between places that need transportation, why not simply give them a lift? But that sort of reasoning never seemed to hold water. There may be vacant housing too, but as soon as you talk about letting the homeless live there, they look at you like you're some sort of a fringe loon.

"Just think of the smell!" Aaron could imagine Lena Biddle saying: "synthetic tobacco vapor and malted fiber-weed liquor. Yuck!"

And so naturally, the autopilot taxis were programmed to consider such moneyless voyageurs as irrelevant carbon blobs, only fit for jettison.

"In other science news, the colonial mission to Mars will again be delayed for more planning and resource deposi-tion before any launch of peopled rockets. The MonDow

Corporation announced pulling its support for a launch, which was planned for execution as early as later this week. MonDow has not commented specifically on why they were pulling their support, citing only safety concerns brought on by recent projections of the long-term viability of the intended seed colony."

Jerry will be disappointed. And his daughter. That Dr. Pernici gave me the willies though. I wonder if Freedom had anything to do with that decision. Hell, what do I care? I'm riding the coattails of fate, now. The Great Train Engineer of Time! Aaron was beginning to entertain grandiose delusions. *More of a caboose though, really.*

He felt he was flying high in the driverless loaner car from MonDow, but Aaron knew he would have to face the fact that his automobile was probably on its way to being melted down for scrap. It was easy to get lost in the moment and forget he was about to show up extra-tardy to a job site where all sorts of higher-ups from the Department of Permaculture and the general public were currently commingling. He had no idea if they had found the Tree or not. If they had found it, he would be a hero and have a little bit less to worry about for money's sake. If not, he would probably be fired. His car was still fucked up either way. But for what it was worth, there he was enjoying the ride.

A billboard caught Aaron's eye from the adiabatic cabin of the auto-piloted loaner car. It contained a simple logo for Gummy Nugs© in pink bubble letters and the address of a headshop that sold their products, *Luke's Vapor Imperium*(sic), *223 5th Avenue, Tampa, FL.*

Aaron thought about how late he was and realized it didn't matter if he showed up a little later still. He checked his tracer to see if he had enough carbon credit in his virtual wallet to afford a vaporizer. Negative five showed in red under his balance statement. *It must be a mistake*, he thought he still had at least a hundred carbon creds. A charge showed up for C125 and the name of the charge was "HIWAY SPEEDER AUTO-BILL." Seemed in his rush to get to work this morning he'd been tagged and debited by a sonar turret. Maybe he wouldn't be purchasing of legal cannabis vaporizer after all. And alt

hough he didn't yet know it, those negative five carbon credits would be the last good money that Aaron Waters would be spending for a long, long time.

CHAPTER 9

"Everybody who has ever worked for a corporation knows that corporations conspire all the time. Politicians conspire all the time, pot-dealers conspire not to get caught by the narcs, the world is full of conspiracies. Conspiracy is natural primate behavior."

-Robert Anton Wilson

Buck D'Aster knew it was going to be a bad day. He'd known since his brief conversation with Burgman at the end of the previous day, before driving home with unfinished business and uncertainties piling up all around him. But what cemented his premonition that morning was the smoldering wreck of a Honda Squire in the divider between the piloted vehicle highway and the DVO lane. Buck knew a bad omen when he saw one.

He was never the sort of man who'd acquired an appreciation for the unknown. Buck was a man who had learned to calculate risk despite an almost genetic aversion to the act of critical thought. His dad had been a heavy equipment operator and retired only to his grave – the smashed-in cab of a log truck. He went off the road to avoid hitting a hunter and crashed headlong 25 yards through a thick young pine grove. Buck had started out running trucks through the woods, when there *were* woods and when trucks were trucks, as a logger during the Last Gasp effort to remove the last of the workable lumber from the dying forests already swamped with fiberweed. He'd worked in the fiber fields for 20 years since then. He'd appreciated the steady work even if it was at a backbreaking pace. Among the things, Buck D'Aster especially did *not* appreciate were unannounced visits by outside authorities, enforcement of arbitrary rules, and visitors from the public. And surprises. Today, he would be getting a taste of a mélange of some of his least favorite things.

If the number of calls he'd fielded the day before was an indicator of the coming day's terribility, it was going to be a record shitstorm. He sipped his coffee extra slowly in the cab of his custom-built off-road truck. It was one of only a few hundred in the country built without navigation or autopilot features and he'd kept it running in good order since the Last Gasp out of pride and stubbornness. One hand on the steering wheel, the other clutching his coffee thermos close to his heart, he made his way steadily down the middle lane neither quick nor sluggish.

His antique iPhone rang on the dashboard. He glanced at it, though there wasn't a chance he would be answering it. Again, it rang and he turned the radio up to override the noise coming off the dash. He decided to skip his morning routine at the regional HQ and head straight to the to where Burgman told him to meet. Burgman and his crew would probably already be out there, along with whoever was calling him and God knows what else. He lit a syntharette with the truck's antique cigarette lighter that he had to personally install. The radio blared as the cab of the truck filled with wisps of bluish aerosol.

"RENT TO OWN! OUR SPECIAL, SMALL BATCH MICRO LOT OF ARTISANAL AUTO TRUCKS ARE FLYING OFF THE LOTS! GUZZLE E85 OR SIP IT SLOW WITH OUR CARBON-SAVING TURBO TECH! CONDITIONS APPLY, DON'T LOSE OUT! CALL OUR CREDIT NEGOTIATING LOAN SHARK: RAGING RON HYDER! ★★PATRIOTIC?! PROVE IT! GET IN YOUR TRUCK AND DRIVE IT –"

Why am I listening to this crap? Buck thought, changing the station.

"–and that's why we say the Oak should be cut. It's a paradox: in order to save our environment, we must destroy certain parts of it. The decision was already made with the introduction of the carbon economy and the demand for more fuel in a fashion that could be sustained indefinitely."

"You're hearing Freedom Vinolte with MonDow joining us this morning on *On Point*. You're listening to NPR. I'm Porter Spandeer. Freedom, what do you say to people who say that the Oak can sequester more carbon than the fiberweed and maybe reverse the climate catastrophe that we're living out today?"

"That sounds a bit radical, don't you think, Porter?" Freedom seemed to scoff; Buck couldn't tell from the radio.

"Do you want to talk about sequestering carbon? Trees make shade. Our beloved fiberweed grows in the beautiful Florida sun. We turn fiberweed into carbon: cold hard cash. I can't even imagine the nightmare of a world in which useless oaks lord over the land and keep us from producing fuel and making money. That's what I would call unsustainable."

"We have a call from Jim in Tarpon Springs. Jim, are you there?"

"Yeah, I'm old enough that I can remember the big old Oaks and I want to say they didn't have to cut them during the Last Gasp and I also wanna say that with today's projected heat index at Severe, we could use more shade from Trees like the Oak they wanna cut today. Save the Oak!"

"Thanks, caller. How do you respond to that perspective, Freedom?

"Look, Porter. I think it's easy to be nostalgic about pristine forests and all that sort of a thing: animals running around, natural shade, leaves, cool breeze, and all that. But we have envirosuits for a reason. There's just no way we can go back to that now. We've run the numbers hundreds of times and there's just too much carbon in the air. It's like if you dropped an egg and wished it would go back to being in a shell. But you can't just pick up a broken egg. It's too late and we need all the fiberweed fuel anyway. By the way, the deepest shade would be found under the now extinct black walnut trees. So, oaks aren't that great to begin with."

"We're here with Freedom Vinolte, executive vice president of MonDow. She's here to defend the fiberweed and the cancellation of the Mars colonial launch, which--"

"Postponement, not cancellation, Porter. We're still going to launch. But I have an announcement that the Pernicis will not be involved. I'm breaking this news here, Porter. There was a vicious attempt on my life this morning. Dr. Pernici and his wife stormed the MonDow corporate office and the coward hit me in the chest point blank with a laser pistol."

"You're kidding... are you alright?"

"No, Porter. It's a shame. I don't think our relationship can recover."

"So he came into your office, what did he s–say?" Porter's voice quavered.

"He said 'we're launching with or without MonDow.' I told him, 'like hell you are. You will launch when we are ready for you to launch.' And he sort of fumbled around in his jacket and clumsily blasted me in the chest and walked off. I didn't know what happened and I guess it was set on stun, or maybe the silencer took the brunt of the projection because I woke up alone on the floor of my office with a headache. And look, Porter, there's soot all over my top!"

Buck smiled and took a deep draught of his coffee. *At least I'm not the only one having a bad day.* He took another gulp of his coffee. He always bought the pure stuff. He spent an inordinate proportion of his wages on coffee. He didn't care.

"Did you call the police? And what's the story of the postponement?"

"Yes, the cops were called and I'm sure they'll undertake a thorough investigation of our break room and generally waste everyone's time. The thing about the postponement Porter is that we have been screwed. Am I allowed to say that on the air?"

"Yes, I think so..."

"There are certain proprietary things I can't tell you, but suffice it to say that the oak tree found by the Department of

Permaculture crew was not supposed to be there. Frankly, I don't care about that stupid tree or what happens to it. I am disappointed for our colonists and astronauts who now have to wait, maybe years, for their lives to take off, if you'll forgive the pun."

"Right, because that Tree indicates something is wrong with … what, exactly?"

"Something is wrong, alright. We just don't know what, yet. I'm surprised everyone is losing it over this."

"And this is *The Zest* on WUSF. It's been years, decades even, since anyone has heard of a wild Tree. The idea seems to rouse the imaginations of many of our listeners. One person wrote in and told us it was the most exciting thing she could remember! Others, young people in particular, can't remember the dying forests. But we seem to, in some sense, associate the death of our forests with the death of an earlier way of living. And it seems that this Tree is a beacon for some, or a portal, to remember better days. What do you say to those people?"

"Porter, something you may not know about me is that I grew up in the FEMA camps. I never knew my real parents. But I was able to get ahead and make something of my life. MonDow is my family now. And we don't have many tree enthusiasts there. We love the fiberweed and we love renewable fuel, perennial jobs, and fields of beautiful green. And we love our country. And we're coming after you, Pernici. But I've gotta go, I'm booked at this stupid pow-wow about the tree in the middle of frickin' nowhere," her voice getting guttural with anger as it spilled into the cab of Buck's truck.

But Buck knew that she had fibbed live on the air. The truth was that Freedom had not come up through the camps. At least, not like the other kids. It was true she never knew her parents, but that was the result of being forced into a twins experiment in epigenetics at birth. Buck too was one of the lost twins. Freedom and Buck's own twin brother were adopted by a wealthy family in the small luxury section of the camp, while Buck and Freedom's twin sister Tricia had been adopted by a poor family. Buck's twin and Freedom herself were the children of the veritable overseers of the great temporary-yet-permanent FEMA camps that now dotted the highways.

The twin known as Freedom told her interviewer that she'd come of age impoverished in an internal displacement camp, perhaps to garner public support for MonDow and the launch. Almost the entire population had been affected by the destruction and rearrangement of the wild world. But she had kept the whole truth hidden. She'd kept that kernel sealed inside. Because if revealed it could pop and destroy her reputation and her career. She'd had everything from new clothes and toys to the best foods: fresh meat and vegetables, whole grains, and fruits and nuts to eat while developing as a child. Propelling her high-powered existence was this secret history, which could ruin her if anyone ever knew that the truth was not rags to riches, but rather riches to filthy riches. And as Buck knew, the only people who knew this were bound to an NDA written by none other than Dr. Eddy Horn, the chief investigator in epigenetics at the University of Florida at the time.

He gritted his teeth and gripped the wheel with a force that whitened his knuckles.

"Freedom Vinolte, everyone. Executive VP of Mon-Dow. Thanks for being with us today, Freedom," Porter said earnestly into the microphone, "It's *On Point*, and I'm Porter Spandeer."

NPR is brought to you by Google TimeRend™. Stretch out your lunch hour or shorten your commute. TimeRend™ is making life Relativity Easier™. And by the Visa retina scanner. 'You were charged for that!'™ ... And by Gummy Nugs©: they're nugs and they're gu--

Buck flipped the volume of the radio to inaudible and drove on in silence. The road and the vibrations created white noise which emanated throughout his vehicle and created a brutally solitary reality tunnel. But there was also hot coffee in its purest form available. He sipped from his antique thermos again. The thermos had gained a unique bouquet from years of coffee residue and just a rinse. It was never scrubbed. There was no one like Buck anymore.

★   ★   ★

Aaron Waters was also in a unique reality tunnel, one that was beginning to take a strange turn. Buck and Aaron were headed to the same place and were within only a couple of minutes of each other on the highway, though neither of them knew it. But while Aaron was already late, Buck wasn't expected for another 15 minutes. In Buck's position, no one noticed if he was gone. He'd been around so long that people at the office didn't ask questions if he didn't even turn up at all. Aaron didn't have that luxury. Aaron was starting to let his guard down, riding merrily along in a car driven entirely by itself. The MonDow car had been a bit ornery, to begin with, but it was at least driving him in the correct direction. He was half-expecting the car to drive him into a lake or slam on the brakes for no reason. But the drive so far had been entirely without incident. So, Aaron didn't react immediately when blue and red lights and a nearly imperceptible siren came up and filled his rear-view mirror with terror.

How do I pull over a driverless vehicle? Aaron wondered in a panic.

His day had already had one highway mishap, and he couldn't spare any adrenaline. He just let the car hold the reins. It knew and pulled over safely. The window rolled down and the engine powered down. He was delivered to authority without a hassle.

He saw the police cruiser slow to a stop in the mirror. Something manlike got out of the vehicle. It looked human, like a regular white-skinned cop with a mustache, but it moved like an animal. It sauntered up to Aaron's car like a wolf wearing the skin of a man. The skin suddenly grew mottled, then darkened to chestnut brown. It had changed to match Aaron's skin color.

Oh, Jesus, he thought. *It's one of the new AI cop drones. An android.*

Aaron never got used to the idea of intelligent machines. The idea creeped him out. Especially when they did human jobs. It made sense, saving the taxpayers' money, but still...

The officer sashayed up to the window and put its synthetic, greasy silicone paws on the door.

Goddamn, this is weird. He has moisture pores. To imitate sweat.

"Lemme see your license, insurance, and proof of franchise," a hidden silicone diaphragm forced air through a complex throat module producing words in a Florida cracker accent at Aaron. Apparently, the skin could change, but the voice and the language remained the same. It was disconcerting, and Aaron was intimidated.

Aaron reached for his wallet and the officer's hand caressed the engraved leather blaster holster on his cheap nylon belt. Aaron realized immediately with the emptiness in his back pocket that he left his wallet in his car -- his dog-dump of a car, which he had left smoldering on the shoulder of this morning's highway.

"I don't have it on me, I left it back with..." he didn't want to admit to abandoning his junk-mobile in the road, even though the license plate was in his name anyway.

"You don't even have your license?" the cop scoffed.

<<Run a scan>> a voice suggested softly, merrily inside Aaron's head.

"Can't you just do a scan?" Aaron pleaded.

"Yeah, alright," the cop acquiesced.

"Aaron Waters, enviro tech for Florida DoP. You could never afford this vehicle with that wage," the machine told him.

The artificial life form jabbed its enervated silicone finger into a hole in the side-view mirror. A sound like a seat belt buckling registered. Aaron sat looking at the police android but the eyes had blanched. There was no one home for a second. And then the officer came to.

"Says you're borrowing this vehicle from MonDow. What business do you, an environmental technician for the State of Florida, have that you're driving one of their cars?"

Aaron thought about Jerry, Freedom, and Lena Biddle. Then he remembered his dead car smoldering in the shoulder. *Better not tell the whole truth.*

<<Say you are taking it through a car wash>> a voice giggled, bubbling to the fray from the subconscious depths of his mind.

"I'm taking it to a car wash for them," he lied.

"Trying to make some extra carbon on the way to work? Smart man," the gullible robot police officer replied.

"I'm so tired of manufactured noodles," Aaron said truthfully, running with it.

"I remember when I was first activated and put through training, I never thought I would ever become a fully functioning android or be employed enforcing the law. But with every failure, I grew stronger and I learned. You also will learn in this way. Drive safely," the law requested of him and traipsed his lousy figure back to his cruiser.

Why wouldn't the cars just drive themselves in to be washed? Aaron thought, trying not to think too loud.

Aaron realized this hole in his lie as he leaned back in the seat of the loaner from MonDow. The cop didn't figure it out or had more important business; because it drove off so fast the tires squealed in Aaron's ears, amid an undeniable ringing of silver bells.

They manufacture the police all out of metal and silicone, and that one still had a muffin top: how bizarre... Aaron couldn't suppress a chuckle as he re-engaged the loaner autopilot vehicle and kicked his feet up on the dashboard. His ears tingled with the weird bell sound and he wanted to reach out and embrace the entire vista of his world and beyond. It wasn't an unpleasant feeling, no doubt he felt powerful, but he was unaccustomed to this power and didn't know what to do with it.

CHAPTER 10

"...of the many kinds of pleasure literature can minister, the highest is the pleasure of the imagination. Since not everyone is capable of experiencing that pleasure, many will have to content themselves with simulacra."

-Jorge Luis Borges,
An Examination of the Work of Herbert Quain

Aaron was by now beginning to accept hearing bells and voices as some sort of unknown complication. Perhaps it was another detail in the bizarre ordeal that his life had become. Even the subliminal suggestions that had just saved him from arrest by a race-shifting police droid, even *that* graceful intervention didn't seem too strange. He chalked it all up to luck. After the Oak incident and everything that had happened since, Aaron was ready to accept anything. He was, after all, sitting in the driver's seat of a newish auto-piloted vehicle after limping around in a decades-old Honda Squire. But the most remote occurrence, he recalled, was that a beautiful and fascinating woman had called him the night before and seemed legitimately interested in getting to know him. He beamed in the freedom that had been afforded him.

Gloria Day on the other hand was dealing with Dr. Horn, who had dropped everything to follow the strange reports that were trickling in to the journals of medicine from researchers and medical scientists around the globe. He'd become obsessed after seeing firsthand the odd case of Aaron Waters, who seemed to have conjured up an actual acorn from the quirky depths of his fume-blasted skull. Or was it that Mr. Waters was putting everyone on? He hated the unknown. Ever since he was a kid when he was called "Ready Eddy" Horn, he always tried to be prepared for anything.

"Are you ready for your afternoon coffee, Dr. Horn?" Gloria asked.

He hated that she felt she had to ask. He wished she would just serve him his coffee and walk away, words unspoken. He looked up from his tracer at her from his desk in the clinic. He was glaring at her. *Through* her.

"Well, are you ready or not? Jesus Christ!" she blurted out.

The doctor sat back and contemplated. This nurse, Gloria, had been employed here for 2 years or so and had never stood up to him like this before. It was a sign of strength and courage, but also a lack of discipline. Or was it a sign that he was building a rapport? He didn't want her to feel she could walk all over him. It was rude of him to ignore her question, but he didn't like being spoken to in such a manner. He was a Doctor, after all.

"Yes, Gloria. I'll want my afternoon coffee. And please don't spit in it. And I told you I want you to get that Aaron Waters guy back in here by whatever means necessary," he told her.

"Whatever," she said in a stable manner and walked out of his office.

She thought about that thoroughly weird and yet totally normal patient she'd phoned up the night before. She wondered why Dr. Horn was so hung up on that acorn guy.

Nurse Day ran over the strange details of the patient again in her head. It had seemed at first like a normal case of heat exhaustion and the related psychosis. But then the acorn in the patient's pocket threw that assumption in the trash. Gloria was pretty sure the acorn was stolen or more likely a fake. But anyone that could procure an acorn, even if it was a convincing fake, must be a powerful person. Acorns were a matter of national security; they didn't just fall out of the sky anymore. In her mind, there were two possibilities and the first being that Mr. Waters and his crew were attempting to subvert the medical system and get unauthorized access to services, or else they were telling the truth. She didn't care either way, but she was still curious, which was the reason she'd called Aaron the night before and not because Dr. Horn told her to.

★   ★   ★

Peradventure Aaron had not made it to work yet, but he was getting there. The piloted vehicle lane sat idling beside him, a blur beyond the bubble of his own private autonomic vehicular universe. He took a deep breath and leaned back in the seat. He was traveling over 100 miles per hour but felt stationary. He closed his eyes and the familiar voice of the Domestic Affairs Drone, or 'DAD' as the complex computer prog was affectionately known, reported from the murky depth of memory:

"An object in motion stays in motion. Newton had to get hit on the head with an apple just to write that down!"

The rushing surroundings passed soundlessly. Hundreds of people encased in lesser technology, including several Squires much newer than his own abandoned model, passed in less than a moment and shrank permanently behind him.

"Now within range of your destination," the voice of the driverless told Aaron.

It seemed to him that he'd come a long way from the relocation camp he was brought up in. He remembered the long rows of tents, the smell of propane and broth in the air. And he remembered long days of DAD instructions. He shuddered to think about putting on the sweaty old virtual reality helmets handed down from kid to kid. Every kid got the same lessons, the same DAD force-feeding them algebra, history, social dynamics, etc. At least they were all subjected to the same thing.

Though he hated hand-me-down gear, he still remembered DAD fondly and was heartbroken when he died at the end of the program. Aaron knew DAD was going to die because the older kids had told him that that's what happens at the end. But somehow, he wasn't ready when the day came that DAD had his "stroke" and wouldn't greet him when he put the greasy VR helmet on anymore. Instead of exuberantly spouting off organic chemistry lessons, he just had that blank look on his wrinkly face with his salt and pepper goatee. His lessons were done and DAD was running a circular script of code so he couldn't say anything anymore. It was so anticlimactic that Aaron wondered if the program was designed that way or if the programmers simply ran out of funding. He didn't even get any congratulations on finishing the program. It seemed like an oversight, like the writers were in a hurry to complete it and get the helmets manufactured. Thinking of this time in his life, Aaron missed DAD and for a second began to feel blue in the cab of the driverless vehicle. That was years ago. But he carried with him this sadness as the vehicle exited the highway, passing a line of parked cars backing up the exit.

There was all manner of vehicles, from police cruisers and ambulances to press vehicles, state vehicles, and lots of unmarked civilian cars. It appeared that some people were trying to make the Oak the story of the century and everyone there had a role to play.

Aaron's car parked itself in a patch of fiberweed mulch and opened the door for him. He got out and it closed itself and locked. He briefly wondered how he'd ever find the car again. Then he wondered how he was going to find his crew, but not for long because soon he heard the sound of a crowd applauding. It sounded like someone was giving a speech 100 yards away, but he couldn't see who through the thick fiber. He followed a path of fresh-cut stalks and the racket got clearer. It sounded like a thousand people or more. He grew anxious that when he stepped out into the clearing a spotlight would be pointed on him. He thought about turning around and getting back on the highway, but his curiosity drew him on down the path and the thought vanished.

CHAPTER 11

"Bob Wilson says 'There are people who possess secret information.' Wrong. There are people who are possessed by secret information."

— **Philip K. Dick,**
The Exegesis of Philip K. Dick

The path opened up onto a fresh clearing that Aaron recognized as the one his crew had finished yesterday. People were sitting and standing awkwardly on piles of fresh mulch and the media teams were streaming footage from different angles. Someone was speaking at a podium and there was a line of official-looking people from various posts and stations off to both sides of it. Everyone else was in a semi-circle forming a ragtag audience of public riffraff, private interests, and government employees not important enough to speak. It was weird for Aaron to see their work site suddenly converted into a media circus. The two worlds had been incompatible: the harsh reality of his work life and the glamour of the five o' clock news were immiscible and yet here they were, dissolving seamlessly together.

Aaron looked around for his crew and didn't see them. He plopped himself down on a warm pile near the outer rim of the crowd. He had decided to stay and watch things progress from there. He was already so late and the circumstances so strange that he reasoned it probably didn't matter what he did at this point.

"What *I* want to know is: Why wasn't my office consulted at the first sign of something that would halt work out here?" the man on the podium's nasal passage intoned from out of his shiny bald head, beading with sweat. The glistening head poked out from a plaid jacket so hideous that it obfuscated attention and kept the audience from being at ease.

"We need to know when, why, and how workers stop work. It's the only way we can provide accurate reports. We can't provide accurate reports if we don't know how, why, and when workers stop. Work stoppage is the number one drain on our tax dollars besides drug and alcohol use, and it's the job of my office to…" he kept speaking, but Aaron stopped listening to the drone of the loudspeakers.

The air was thick with fiber haze. *So odd*, Aaron thought, *to be out here with all these people. They aren't built to be out in this heat and humidity. There's no wifi or electrical outlets. They could lose access to their tracer and get lost.*

"I'll wrap this up because I know there are a lot of speakers today and I value your time. I thank you all for listening to me. I will conclude by saying that it is up to all of us to hold our government workers accountable for the money we pay them. If they find the Oak, I hope they do whatever will bring the most money in to make up for the lost time and money that it has inflicted upon our sacred budget. And I will also add that the Bureau of Efficiency in Government accepts donations. Thank you all very much and Godspeed in your investigation, goodbye!"

He left the podium with a loud microphone bump. There was an audible sigh of relief and stirring in the crowd as the man left the makeshift stage.

"Okay, that was Chancellor Rand Fornhinder from the Bureau of Efficiency in Government, which we all affectionately call BEG. Thank you, Chancellor," a man with a headset mic said addressing the crowd, with people struggling to hold in their laughter.

"Let's see. Next, we have ...," he paused briefly to strike out Fornhinder's name on the list and read the next entry, "it's the Director of the Society of Geomancy, Harold Wong."

A man approached the stage. He was short and skinny for an American, a youngish-looking man, yet his short hair visibly graying in streaks behind his temples. His sunglasses were oval to the point of insectoid-looking. Perhaps Wong knew this and chose his accessories purposefully. The slight man had also dressed in a brilliant green silk suit, making some in the audience think he looked like a grasshopper.

"Thanks to you sir, Master of Ceremony. I'm with the Society for Geomantic Affairs, and we're not a bureaucracy. Not unrelatedly, thank you to Chancellor Rand for leaving the stage. Haha!" he paused for laughter, "Hail!!"

He seemed buoyant despite the oppressive heat. The way he spoke commanded the attention of the audience, and a silence as powerful as thunder washed over them all.

A moment passed as he surveyed the gathering.

Aaron shifted uneasily on his warm mulch pile, which he shared with two strangers. He guessed from their countenance and their dress that they were from the moneyed leisure class. They were of the ilk that possessed the idle time and the resources to involve themselves when something like a Tree discovery cropped up. They felt it prestigious to be in the orbit of such matters. Aaron looked at his worn work clothes and shrank back to look up at the cloudswept sky.

"Hey, idiot!"

A familiar voice cracked in his ear and someone slapped him on the shoulder. It was Bulkowitz. He'd broken the hypnosis of Wong. And the whole crew was with him: Joey D., Burgman, and Pete Barbour. They'd all snuck up on him somehow. Aaron felt mad, then embarrassed, but then resigned himself to indifference within a matter of seconds.

"Late for your big day? So surprising," Pete said sarcastically and smiled at him.

"Don't worry," Burgman told him, "You aren't fired. Yet!" he laughed heartily.

"You haven't missed anything. It's just been these public balloon-heads all morning," Bulkowitz related.

As if on cue and perfectly on time Buck D'Aster shuffled up the path, hands in his pockets. He gravitated to the crew naturally.

"What a goddamn circus," he remarked. "Hey Waters, where's that Oak of yours? All this commotion and no Tree, what gives?"

The two bourgies whose pile Aaron shared had were growing visibly uncomfortable with the number of working-class men in their vicinity and fled for better-bred company, almost escaping undetected.

"Who are your friends, Waters?" Joey asked, pointing at them: "You think you're too good to sit with your own crew now that you're a certified Tree spotter?"

The crew laughed. The exchange lightened the mood and created a conjunct feeling of belonging among them. They all settled in on the pile and sat for a listen, the speaker already under way with his speech.

"It's accurate to say the world as we now know it is a quasi-accidental projection of material information which has arisen from past conflicts of a political and economic nature," he told them all.

"The current state of the world consists almost solely of human interventions, but this was not always the case," he said and paused to drink water from a strange metal canteen.

He continued, "We must act as if we have inherited a set of systems which regulates and controls the inputs and outputs of the entire world, from birth to death, from microbe to ecosystem, from atom to molecule to organism to planet and perhaps someday to the harnessing of the power of the stars themselves. Every sunbeam predicted and accounted for."

The audience, hypnotized, sat dumb in the dusty mulch.

"What the fuck is he talking about? Wong? More like WONK!" Bulkowitz hammed, making Joey laugh as he was promptly shushed by nearby media personnel.

"Yes," the man in the fly green suit affirmed: "Yes. AND," Wong emphasized, "That is perhaps only just the *top* layer. For we are now learning that reality may work like the hologram transmitter on your tracers. We may have much less control than we think. In fact," he stopped and looked around. He looked at the ground, at the sky, and deep into the horizon, a sense of urgency coming over his face.

"What the fuck is he doing?" Bulkowitz asked, without cynicism and what sounded to Aaron like fear bleeding through.

"We are all in danger here," Wong stated matter-of-factly and braced the podium as the crowd stirred.

"Danger? What does he mean?" a nearby woman in front of a media stream asked her producer.

"For safety's sake we need to clear the area here immediately," the geomancer spoke ominously but with intention and left the podium promptly.

Mr. Wong walked in the direction of the path and out towards the road. The MC bobbled words, not expecting anything like this to occur:

"Ahh, ladies and gentlemen please remain, ah, in your seats, or if you are standing, ahhh, please remain calm. That was the Director of the Society for Geomantic Affairs," he told the crowd.

Mr. Wong continued to walk out of the clearing, followed by a handful of followers.

"He's gone!" Burgman cheered.

"Should we just ... go too?" Joey asked, praying internally for a shortened day.

Burgman's boss, Buck, was on the schedule to speak at the podium later about how fiberweed works and how

Trees used to be. He wasn't looking forward to it. In any case, the crew decided to stay at least until Buck had spoken.

"Next, we'll hear from the Commissioner of the Florida Department of Permaculture, Kevin Scalder."

A young man in an expensive, normal-looking suit walked to the stage. He didn't look like a grasshopper.

"Hello. Many of you know me. We took this," he gestured to the surrounding swaths of fiberweed, "and we turned it into energy. That was what created our Department but it won't be the end of it. We have plans in place, plans that I can't speak of now, that will create jobs and keep Americans in carbon for the next 100 years. But the reason I'm here is to discuss the tree," Mr. Scalder spoke matter-of-factly from a prepared speech.

"Now, all of us look back fondly on the trees. And many of us wish things were different. But the scientific truth of the matter is that the trees and their timber were unsustainable. The weed, though at first glance appeared to us as a curse, we have reimagined into a blessing. Because as we learned, the fiberweed sequesters more carbon and produces more resources than the trees. And we now know that we are better able to utilize these resources to the benefit of all American people. So, we don't mourn the loss of the trees. We applaud their demise and pray that the Tree that was supposedly discovered yesterday turns out to be a hoax. Thank you," he finished reading from a piece of paper, folded it up, and left the podium unceremoniously.

"Okay, great. Next, we will hear from Freedom Vinolte, executive vice president of MonDow Corporation," the somewhat flustered MC told the audience.

There was some very sparse applause as the six-foot blonde woman took the podium.

"Yeah, thanks. Whoever you are. I've got a Ph.D. by the way, which no one seems to be getting today. Anyway," she looked out at the indifferent crowd indifferently.

You could hear a giant grasshopper chirping in the distance. People were shuffling about but there was no more movement towards the exit.

"Rubisco. RuBisCO!" she called out awkwardly.

The audience was baffled. Aaron and Buck were among the more vexed in the crowd because one had just seen her earlier in the morning and one had just heard her on the radio. But here she was before them, making no sense.

"What'd she say?" Pete asked.

Everyone had by now forgotten the bizarre exit of geomancer Harold Wong.

"Ribulose One-Five Bisphosphate Carboxylase Oxygenase. It's the whole freakin' reason we're here today, folks. Don't listen to that abominable schlub Kevin; the real reason we're here is because of Rubisco. By the way, thanks for the fuel tax, Kevin. We all appreciate how much you claim to do for us while fleecing us."

Laughs percolated through the crowd. Kevin Scalder turned beet red.

"Anyway, Rubisco is the most abundant protein on the face of the Earth and it's the best way to chemically reduce the oxidation state of carbon in carbon dioxide and link those atoms together en masse into more complex carbon. It's also extremely inefficient, at least relatively speaking. Try telling this to the terminal boob heading up the Bureau of Inefficiency. I mean really try it: he'll send you a report on an employee named Ruby Schofield. They call her Scho' for short. Ruby Scho. I'm not kidding; I've seen her employee file. Apparently, similar to Rubisco, she's reliable but not intrinsically motivated. Anyway,"

A handful of people chuckled in the audience and someone coughed loudly.

"I just heard her on NPR in the truck driving over here," Buck said, "It's like she's in two places at once! How can that be?"

"Anyway, look. There are a lot of people here who care, or pretend to care, about the natural world and that's fine, whatever. There's a reason our money is based on carbon. It's the most important element in this cosmic locale. And all this fiberweed?" she gestured to the landscape surrounding them. "Let me tell you, there won't be any trees, won't be any cute wild animals until someone figures out the answer to the question I'm about to ask. And there's no idiot-friendly way to pose it, so put your helmets on."

Aaron looked to his left and right at Buck, Burgman, and the rest of the crew. They were all at full attention to Freedom.

"Okay, we've all been through DAD's middle school intro to organic chemistry spiel. How do you get a carbon atom from a fully oxidized to a reduced state without expending any energy? -You can't, it's... highly unlikely, to put it mildly. We are currently allowing a slow-as-tar enzyme, Ruby Scho, to synthesize sunlight and air into sugar, then let it rot in piles until we come along and distill it into fuel-grade ethanol. The first man or woman to figure out a way to fix Rubisco, or find its replacement, will not only be famous for the next 100 generations, but they will also be the richest person ever to live on the face of the Earth. Until that day, I guarantee you that-"

But before she could finish Freedom was cut off by a deep rumble which caused the podium in front of her to fall forward. She barely caught herself before tumbling off the stage. Aaron saw her speak into her wrist. The audience could feel the tremor.

"What the hell is *that!?*" Joey D. cried.

The sound of a helicopter was closing in. Aaron saw a crack in the ground forming next to them and pointed at it. It opened and closed in sync with the rumbling. The ground also seemed to be liquefying.

"Holy Shit!" Pete and Burgman said in unison.

The crack grew and began to divide. It headed straight for the upturned podium as the crowd split and some poor soul stumbled and fell deep within the terra.

The helicopter was now visible and approaching the crowd. Freedom dashed under it, and a rope unfurled. She hoisted herself to safety as the rest of the crowd panicked and scattered.

The fissure began to multiply into further cracks. Half a dozen more onlookers fell in before they could get to safety.

The crew and Buck watched from the periphery, having been slowly moving back towards the road, until Pete Barbour yelled:

"Run!!"

They darted through the weedy fiber, punching the great stalks aside and cutting their arms and legs on the sharp, dead leaf blades.

They could hear in the background people screeching and wailing, as the great yawning chasm of the Earth swallowed some more of them whole, media gear and all. There was nothing anyone without a personal helicopter on standby could do.

Buck showed up just as everyone was leaving. He hadn't gotten ten yards from his truck when he spotted the crew pop out of the thick weed.

But Buck had known it was going to be a bad day. He didn't predict it would be a 'bottomless pit' sort of day, but if that meant not having to speak to the public and possibly leaving work early, it would seem his outlook for the day was improving.

Once they felt they'd reached a safe distance, the crew slowed to a walking pace. Aaron checked his tracer. A fly crawled across the cracked screen. He tried to flick it away but his finger went right through it. The fly was holographic.

Damn, this thing is so old it's growing its own flies! he thought pathetically to himself.

The thought didn't last, as he realized the fly had been programmed for his amusement, or to motivate him to purchase a new tracer. Obviously, he couldn't afford a new one

as he'd had to buy his current one used. It'd had a crack
on the screen when he got it. Now the software on it was
turning against him, making up hologram flies and doing
who knows what else to get him to discard it and purchase
a brand-new one. *Was the crack even real?*

Despite this, he managed to see he'd missed a couple of
calls from Gloria, the nurse from yesterday. Apparently, she
didn't leave messages.

"Hey, you guys mind if I return this call real quick?" he
asked of the others with him.

"Yeah, that's cool. We'll just be up here running for our
lives while you catch up with your chums," Mark Bulkowitz told him from up the trail.

"Go ahead," Burgman, the crew lead, said authoritatively.

"New girlfriend?" Pete winked.

The tracer whirred electronically in his ear as he held it
to his head. Aaron's head was spinning as the Earth settled
behind them. He struggled to catch his breath. He felt a
strange vertigo, like when stepping off an elevator.

"Hello?" came the voice through the phone.

"Hi, Gloria?"

"Hi!"

"Hi, this is Aaron."

"Yeah, I know."

"...I saw you called before?"

"Yeah, I wanted to see if you could get dinner tonight."

Her voice was warm and inviting. Without a thought of
his negative credit, he replied:

"Sure! Where do you want to meet?"

"Um, we can meet at the bus stop near my place. I live in St. Pete. Is that okay?"

"Yeah, sure. See you later, like 6 or so?"

"Yeah, that works. I'll text you the details. See ya then!"

Wow! He thought. He thought he was a lucky guy for a few moments. And then he recalled that he'd suffered a heat stroke, seen an Oak mirage, survived an exploding car, and barely escaped an earthquake/sinkhole situation all within the past 24 hours. And also, that he had no money or prospects for a better position. *Whatever, maybe that's what Gloria finds attractive in a man!* He laughed audibly to himself. His tracer bleeped, indicating Gloria had sent him an address.

"What's up? Got a hot date?" Joey D. asked from the rear.

"Yeah," is all he said.

"Did anyone see Freedom Vinolte take off? I mean she bolted! Like, she must've called that 'copter after that Geo-loon spoke," Ralph addressed the crew.

"Yeah, I saw her. She was *out!* Like donuts at a cop convention!" Buck quipped.

"That chick is everywhere. I saw her this morning, over at er... uh," Aaron stumbled, remembering he wasn't going to mention the loaner car he'd gotten at MonDow.

"Yeah, well I heard her on the radio on the ride out here. She definitely gets around," Buck said.

They were approaching the end of the trail. Aaron could see the work truck, Buck's truck, and of course his loaner driverless rig. He blushed with frustration because he hadn't thought about what to do in the coming situation. *Would he pretend the car wasn't his and just get in the work truck? What would happen if he didn't return the car?*

"Where's your car, Waters?" Burgman asked him directly.

"Oh, I uh... got this rental car over here," he said, trying desperately to deflect. "Aren't we going to talk about the giant sinkhole we just got away from?"

"What, that driverless joint over there? That old piece of a turd? You're lucky you even made it here! You're probably lucky it's so old; it's probably missed that latest virus that's been hitting the DV computer systems the last couple of days. What happened to your other turd-mobile?" said Joey Dimanche.

"I don't know," Aaron told Joey, hoping he wouldn't say any more things.

"Well, it beats that ancient Squire you've been dragging your sorry ass to work in, I tell you what. The State should've paid you to take that fuckin' thing off the road years ago," Joey continued.

"Hey, watch your language with all these people around. We're not at the garage yet," Burgman told Joey and turning to Buck D'Aster he said:

"Buck, should we all head back to district HQ or just go back to our garage and go home?"

"It's your call, Chief. I'm going to HQ to lay low and cover my ass. If you want, I'll tell them that you're doing tools maintenance for the rest of the day, that might keep anyone from bugging you."

Aaron had been expecting to lose his job today, but he reasoned that they couldn't fire him on the same day of a natural disaster. He wasn't keen on leaving with the crew in the work truck and trying to get a ride back later, so he sort of shuffled to his loaner car and waited there.

"Alright, thanks, Buck. Aaron, meet us at the garage," Burgman said.

Aaron nodded and hopped into his ride. He struggled again with the controls, but he'd learned some shortcuts since the last time he attempted to operate the DV. The road to the highway was clogged with people trying to escape the sinkhole. Every hundred feet it seemed another emergency vehicle went by and shut down the flow. But once Aaron got to the highway, he'd never seen it so vacant. There were hardly any cars anywhere. *Kinda spooky*, he thought.

Aaron made it to the garage before the rest of the crew and so he had his loaner car pull off and wait on the shoulder until Ralph got there with the keys to the gate. Once they were all there, it was the same old routine. Wash the armor for 20 minutes and shoot the breeze for two hours. Except with half an hour left, Ralph Burgman called Aaron back to the makeshift office, apart from the rest of the crew.

"Aaron, I hate to say it man, but you're losing your job. There's nothing I can do. They log the hours and the admins can see that you've been 20 minutes late every day."

Aaron remembered installing the Florida DoP app on his tracer when they hired him. They had known when he was there and for how long, and every time he was more than 15 minutes late.

"I covered for you as much as I could. You've been a great worker for most of these past two years and the crew won't be the same without you," Burgman concluded.

"Yeah, I figured. I guess I've been needing to make a change for a while now. I appreciate all you've done and for the opportunity," Aaron responded amicably.

But in his heart, he was filled with dread and fear. Which he found surprising, considering he'd been expecting to be fired for at least a couple of weeks now. And he couldn't blame Burgman or the rest of the crew. They'd all been showing up on time.

CHAPTER 12

"Caveat emptor."

—Marcus Aurelius

Aaron Waters must've been the least fortunate lucky guy, or else the luckiest unfortunate man to ever live. He would perhaps never be aware of either of these possibilities. By all accounts, his life had recently been changing for the worse. Until earlier in the day he'd held a low wage job as an environmental technician where he'd spent the last two years cutting fiberweed and fighting fiber fires in south Florida. And yet, for all that he'd labored to maintain the ethanol-producing fields of the mysterious supergrass, he had been just barely managing to keep fuel in his 20-year-old Honda Squire. He'd just lost job with rent due in a week. Chalk it up to human irrationality or emotions, but Aaron's psyche was adapting. He was beginning to realize that anything could be better than even eight more hours of the sun's heat radiating inside an armor suit, or the toxic sap of the obliterated weed chunks leaking through its cracks. No, he didn't have the money for rent. Not even close. But he was somehow more worried about how he was going to take beautiful Gloria Day out for dinner. And remembering that a malfunctioning driverless vehicle had totaled his car this morning (not covered by his insurance), he wondered how he was going to get to see her at all. He contemplated these things while the autonomous MonDow car taxied him away from the garage he'd spent every morning trying to get to on time for the past two years.

After leaving work he was dropped off by his driverless loaner car in downtown St. Petersburg near where Gloria lived, 25 miles by crow from his apartment on the outskirts of Tampa. And after spending a good portion of the day wondering how long he could get away with keeping the car, he watched the damn thing drive itself off empty. He sat on a bench and fought off the urge to get back to Tampa somehow, reminding himself there was nothing there for him but an apartment full of dirty clothes and stale bread in the kitchen. Then he paced around the block a few times, anxious about how he could make a decent impression on Gloria tonight with no money.

Gloria was a nurse. She made a comfortable living and probably rode a driverless every day. Then here comes Aaron smelling like hay and gym socks, wanting to take her out for a nice night on the town with no car and no money? Aaron wasn't very charismatic, even at his best, and right now he felt like crawling down a manhole to hide.

It wasn't the *worst* idea. He was starting to seriously consider becoming a St. Pete sewer dweller, when down the block he spotted the ALLCAPS pink bubble letters of a strange-looking new store sign: GUMMY NUGS© CO. He recognized the name from yesterday when his co-worker Joey Dimanche, or more precisely his *former* co-worker, made him try a blast from one of their vaporizer pens. Aaron had very much enjoyed the flavor and cerebral effects of the herbal whiff. But then he got heat stroke, hallucinated that he'd seen a wild Oak Tree where one hadn't stood for two decades, and started a national debate on what to do with the apparently non-existent tree. The plus side of that debacle was that he got to meet a wonderful nurse named Gloria who had treated his dehydration with such a canny bedside manner.

"Don't go in there," someone said from below.

"Huh?" Aaron intoned, looking down at the raspy-voiced stranger.

The unshaven man was drinking a tall can of beer from a paper bag. He had a jar out and a cardboard sign that said, "Why Lie? Need Carbon 4 Ethanall" in red sharpie.

"No one knows what they put in those new vapes," the man cleared his throat, "they say it's some proprietary blend, but it's just a new drug. That's how they've drummed up so much buzz. Me and my buddies think it's a government trick to get us all brainwashed."

"Have you tried it? The vapor tastes nice and I enjoyed the effects. But I do think it made me sick," Aaron responded to the man on the street.

"Yeah right. You're probably one of *them!*" the man said as he gestured at Aaron accusingly.

He's obviously just paranoid, Aaron thought to himself and walked away.

With time to kill before he was due to meet Gloria, Aaron set off toward the big pink sign. Suddenly he caught a huge whiff of barbecue labmeat and thought about getting a snack of street food. Instead, he pressed on to GUMMY NUGS©. If he couldn't afford rent, or dinner tonight, then he reasoned he shouldn't waste money he didn't have on a snack, which would last a solitary moment and leave him hungry again anyhow. Plus, maybe it would impress Gloria if he got a vaporizer pen.

He walked through a pair of automatic doors into the store as cool air blasted in his face. He felt immediate relief from the humidity and heat of the street. In the store, it didn't smell like street food. It smelled sterile. He looked around at the décor, a couple of fake plants, and some jewelry cases featuring the different styles of vaporizer pens. At first, there was no one around, but presently someone appeared from behind a curtain.

"Hi, welcome to Gummy Nugs. Last week's flavors are 15% off," the youngish attendant recited faithfully before looking down at an info stream on the cash register.

A calming brand of musak played over the speakers just loud enough to drown out the noise of the street. The attendant took a rip off a vape pen and exhaled the fat puffy clouds towards Aaron. She did so without looking away from the feed. To Aaron, the vapor smelled fruity. It reminded him of Joey's pen and the Tree and the trip to urgent care.

"Hi," Aaron said sheepishly.

The attendant didn't respond. Aaron looked around at the vaporizers. All of them cost more than he had in his bank account, which was less than nothing.

"Do you have any discounts besides last week's flavors? These are all pretty pricey."

The cashier looked up and met Aaron's gaze. Without skipping a beat, she told him, "Look dude, our company produces a patented blend of genetically modified hemp and hops hybrid flower oils. Do you know how hard it is to get farmers to grow hemp these days? They all want to grow corn or wheat because they're what the pesticides and herbicides are designed for. It wouldn't be worth it at all if it weren't for the fact that marijuana is illegal," the attendant spoke back to him with astounding impatience.

"No, I don't know that," Aaron replied, now intimidated and confused. Slowly he backed away towards the door.

"Sorry," the attendant said with a sigh, "we've got the DEA breathing down our necks demanding samples of every batch, our margins are ridiculously low to begin with, and no one wants to pay full price for anything. I just don't know how we're going to make it."

"Oh, are you the owner?" Aaron said.

"Yep," she said, "I'm Jane Franklin, patent holder and owner of Gummy Nugs brand. We farm out our manufacturing to the big guys, so if you're thinking of asking for a job think twice."

"Oh, okay. I'm Aaron Waters and I'm newly unemployed, but I wasn't going to ask for a job. I worked cutting fiberweed for the last two years," he told her.

She didn't even look up from her info stream, so Aaron assumed that didn't impress her.

"So, what's in this stuff, anyway?"

Jane rolled her eyes, sensing she wasn't dealing with a big spender and she would have to represent her brand for free.

"It's a blend of terpenes and esters as well as cannabidiol or CBD, which is still technically legal, in just the right proportions to affect the senses and the mind. By the way, I did my dissertation at USF on vaporized botanical compounds and their effects on focus, stamina, and mentation."

"Huh. So why hemp?"

"Because it's a plant that's a veritable chemical factory and it only runs on dirt, air, water, and sunlight! And because it was easy to genetically modify. And other reasons."

"Okay. Well thanks," Aaron said, pretending to look around the store some more.

Jane looked him up and down and then looked back at her info stream. She was sure he wouldn't be buying anything, and that Aaron was just making a slow exit as fast as he could.

He recalled in a flash the giant Oak Tree and his episode and thought about bringing it up, but then thought better of it. He thought of asking her about vaporized fiberweed and whether it could cause hallucinations or heat stroke. Finally, he pushed himself to the door after carefully deliberating whether he would or wouldn't mention his experience.

"Here, take this," Jane finally said as he approached the exit.

Aaron turned around and saw Jane sterilizing the vaporizer she had been using with an alcohol wipe.

"Tell your friends to come buy my vapes," she told him earnestly as he took the pen from her, "And come back when you have some money, for crying out loud!"

"Thanks! Wow, I really appreciate it," he told her.

She smiled a hard little half-smile and broke out a fresh new vaporizer for herself.

Taking a huge drag on his brand-new secondhand vape pen, Aaron exhaled a big fat, creamy cloud and walked to the exit quicker than before. The first door opened as he neared and he stepped through it without hesitating. Jane Franklin watched him walk out of her store. But the paranoid homeless guy was keeping tabs and never witnessed Aaron come out of GUMMY NUGS© CO. And that's because he never did leave the GUMMY NUGS© CO.

When Aaron Waters reached the second pair of automatic doors, they refused to open. He waved his hand in front of the sensor and a red light blinked with acknowledgment of his existence. He thought maybe it was closing time and it had locked automatically. Or that it was broken or some other issue, and he looked for a manual exit. There was no other door except the one back into the shop and feeling a bit silly he approached that door. But it too refused to budge. He tried to look through the glass to motion to Jane to come help him, but the glass was now frosted. He couldn't see anything beyond the small room in which he now found himself trapped.

A feeling of hopelessness engulfed him, but it didn't last because he felt he was moving. As sure as when an elevator lurches, he felt he was now ascending. Looking down, the floor was different. He remembered a black rubber mat before, now it was what seemed to him to be made of a solid plastic material, or maybe it was metal. The doors too had changed, their windows were opaque and when

Aaron tried waving his hand in front of the motion sensor it wouldn't blink anymore. He searched desperately for a means of orienting himself. His head was spinning: *what the hell is going on?*

Finally, he found a window. There was a tiny crack in the corner where the caulking had come loose. He picked at the rubbery sealant and thought he had gotten a grip on it and pulled. Air rushed in through the new hole. He managed to position his eye to look through it. He couldn't believe what he was seeing: the city of St. Pete was rapidly flying away beneath him. There was no evidence of a trail of exhaust so Aaron thought perhaps one of those huge construction cranes had lifted up the entrance to the store. But as time went by, he came to know there was no crane, no crane at all. There was no crane because he could now see the Gulf of Mexico. And in a moment as Tampa Bay retreated beneath him, he could see all of Florida, its silver-green fiber seas interrupted by the grayness of pavement and cities. Soon the entire southern United States, Cuba, Mexico, the Caribbean, and Central and South America were in view. At some point, he noticed that there was no more air rushing in through the hole. In an impossibly short amount of time, he was leaving the Earth and his ears hadn't even popped. He weighed the potential he was hallucinating again. *What if that cloud of vapor Jane had gifted him had affected his mind?* Maybe, like last time, he'd wake up with people surrounding him, and he'd be on the way to see beautiful Gloria Day at urgent care again. That was a comforting thought and soon Aaron's panic stopped snowballing and he melted.

Accepting his complete lack of control in this situation, he lay down on the floor and re-activated Jane's vaporizer. It had become his anchor, the one thing he could control. He inhaled great lungs of the GMO hemp chemicals and relaxed there on his ground in the sky. He even had himself a little chuckle, fully expecting to wake up in the arms of a beautiful nurse.

But as luck would have it, he was now entirely out of reach of Gloria Day or any other human being. Nevertheless, it turned out his relaxation was a good strategy for the position in which he would soon find himself. Panic can be lethal for a game animal. And though he was almost wholly unaware of it, that's exactly what the human being known as Aaron Waters was: quarry. Cool as a cucumber, he hummed to himself some old song and hardly noticed when his room in the sky stopped moving. Faintly he heard metal-on-metal and noticed that at some point the door's motion sensor light turned to blinking green. Looking out his little peep-hole, he saw only stars. No Earth, no moon, no planets. No sun in sight. Just plenty of nameless little stars, hopelessly distant. Then the door opened without a prompt. That's about when Aaron felt the adrenaline. It felt remote since he had rapidly devoured almost the entire CBD/terpene cartridge in the vape pen given to him by Jane, bless her soul. The adrenaline just sort of hung there in the background. His muscles weren't tense like other times he'd been pumped up with his fight-or-flight response.

What the hell? What do I do now? Aaron's thoughts spiraled.

<<Don't panic, dude! We'll get you out of here>> a friendly voice in his head related.

Oh, good God. Now I'm hearing voices. What a way to go: lose my mind, blast off into space and hear voices. He thought maybe, in reality, he was foaming at the mouth in a full-blown seizure on the sidewalk in front of GUMMY NUGS©.

<<<You're not crazy, just a little scared. And pale, too!>>> another voice came through and broke into laughter.

Aaron could hear telepathic snickering. *Jesus, how many of you are there? What is this anyway?*

<<<Haha! Okay, listen up 'Air-and-Waters,' ha, we can save your life. Again...>>

<<...For the 13th time>>

<<< but you have to follow our instructions. You are in grave danger, Aaron Waters. **Graaave daaanger!**>>>

<<Wooo! So spooky>>

What is this, a prank?

"Hello? Joey? Is that you?" he said out loud.

"Hey it's Joey c'mon bro!" a voice responded from outside the open door in a Joeyish manner. It wasn't very convincing.

<<Shut up, idiot. You're going to get yourself zapped!>>

<<<Yeah, dum-dum. Do you want to end up with your tenderloins frozen? And your hams, and sweet, savory human belly? Mmm, Aaron bacon>>

Oh my God, I've lost it. What the--

<<Alright, enough funny business, Aaron. You've got to end the hunt. Yell at the top of your lungs that you see the hunters and the game is over.>>

<<<Yell it, Aaron. Yell it now or you will die. Painfully. I mean eventually, you'll die, but you'll have to withstand

some pretty weird stuff first. Have you ever been biologically hardwired to an information database? It's pretty jarring. I mean, some people like it, but...>>>

<<Shut up, dude>>

<<<Why? We already broke cover to save his ass, I might as well be candid>>>

<<Because you're confusing him and it's jeopardizing the mission. He doesn't know what any of this is. And I don't want to go back to overt chronomic hostage training, do you?>>

<<<Pfft, whatever. Go ahead, Air'n'waters>>>

Having these unidentified, invisible entities argue in his head was the strangest sensation Aaron had felt since the first time he'd mistakenly mulched a giant grasshopper in the fiberweed – the broken legs kicking, the feelers whirling, the slimy concoction of appendages and goop covering his entire body. But that was just a disgusting and persistent coating on his brush armor, while this current situation seemed interior to his mind. He wasn't faring very well against the confusing conversation unfolding inside his head.

"Dude, what the fuck?" he said out loud.

He looked around the empty room and out the open doors. A dimly lit corridor extended as far as he could see. It was quiet now, quieter than anything he'd experienced on the crowded Earth. He felt like there was cotton in his ears. He could see his pulse in the periphery of his vision. Thinking about stepping out of the room made him nervous, but thinking about shouting about hunters and the game being over made him feel silly. Confused and scared, he tried to talk himself down.

Get over it, man. He told himself. *Maybe the voices are right and you are in danger. If someone or something is hunting you it won't matter if you yell. Maybe that's when the joke will end and the fiberweed brush crew will jump out and reveal their monkeyshine.*

He decided to go for it.

"Hey!" he said loudly.

Moments passed in silence.

"HEY!" he yelled.

"Aaron? Help! I can't see you!" the voice of Gloria projected from the dark hall.

<<<You're an idiot if you think that's your date>>>

He thought he heard a rustling. Blurry figures quivered in the dim corridor connecting to his sky room.

"Game's over! I see hunters!" he said, feeling ridiculous.

"Well, aren't you special?" a voice spoke with a gargling mucus excess.

Blurred lines formed along the side of the corridor outside the room. Three figures developed out of perfect photonic camouflage and revealed themselves. At the same time, two entities flew out from behind Aaron's head. He assumed those were the embodiment of the voices he'd heard and drew some relief from the fact that he wasn't just imagining the situation. Although perhaps not as much relief as if it had all been a practical joke. Because apparently entities were living in his head and they were just now making themselves visible.

"What the hell? You ruined our hunt! That's against the law! Hunter harassment!" one of the figures said, obviously annoyed.

<<Actually this individual is in our custody and not a legitimate quarry>> one of the hovering thingies projected telepathically to all parties.

Time seemed to slow down as Aaron looked closely at the two beings hovering just feet from his head. They looked like floating babies – fucked up cyborg babies, floating perhaps through telekinesis – big-headed, tiny-bodied, grotesque humanoid machine offspring that had ostensibly just saved his life from the dimly lit extraterrestrial human-hunters. Aaron tried desperately to wake up from this nightmare.

<<<We can hear what you're thinking about us Aaron. Haha!>>> the other one said in Aaron's head.

"Bullshit. Where's his collar? We had him fair and square," one of the hunters stepped towards the room where Aaron stood shaking with his two apparent bodyguards.

<<<The hell you did, he saw you! You will now take us all back to his appropriate time and space>>>

"Oh for the sake of Heat! Will you please stop this charade? You Magi are always trying to get us to bring them home," another of the hunters complained. It continued, "I say, who cares if he saw us? We caught him in our trap, fair as a funky fart, and you want us to take him back because he laid eyes on us? This is so typical, more concern for this stupid human's emotions and fragile, so-called 'mind' than with the progress of the neuro-integrated networks."

<<Hey, rules are rules. You know them better than we do. Do you want to keep him? Fine. But you'll get labeled as poachers and hunted by your own kind>>

Aaron caught a hideous glimpse from the dull light coming out of the room. There beyond the threshold of the room, three monsters stood holding weighted nets. They had leathery skin and great big teeth like tigers. Their eyes were perched upon stalks, like a snail's. They wore one-piece skintight suits of graphene-gray, with power packs on their backs. Their feet were bare, with three big toes almost like an elephant's. He marveled at their crusty toenails which didn't seem congruous with a space-faring civilization.

"Someday, it is you Magi who will be hunted. And then, *we* will make the rules!" one of the monsters spoke up.

<<<Probably not, chief>>>

"We'll leave him. But we're not spending the energy to get you all back home. Fuck you," one of the hunters told them and gave a bras d'honneur.

Then their physical environment began to rearrange.

Aaron still wasn't used to the telepathic speech yet, much less intergalactic temporal transport, so he barely noticed when his surroundings began to melt and fade. For a moment he was floating in space alone, with no way to reference up from down. The room was gone and so were the monsters. Though ostensibly the Magi were still there, not visibly but in his head.

<<Guess you're with us now, dude!>>

<<<Or rather, we're with you>>>

<<Where do you want to go?>>

<<<When do you want to be there??>>>

"Alright, hang on a second. I need a debrief," Aaron started to say but the Magi had already begun to sing him a limerick:

<<<*There once was a man called Aaron*>>>
<<*Whose affairs upon him were wearin'*>>
<<<*He walked into Nugs*>>>
<<*Got picked up by Slugs*>>
<<<*The Magi again have un-snared 'im!*>>>
<<Hey! That was pretty good>>
<<<Not bad, not great. We'll do better next time>>>

"Okay, what is going on? Who, or what, were those hunters?"

<<Them? They were just the Hunters>>

<<<They like hunting. And neurons. For their network. They have a civilization to run, you can't hate them too much for too long. But *we* do. We hate them forever>>>

He looked around. There was only starry sky in every direction, Aaron looked at his feet and found they were not there.

<<Don't pout, it's just dark out>>
<<<What a feat, you still have feet>>>

"I don't understand what you are or why we are here."

<<Classic human complaint>>
<<<Should we give him the three questions?>>>
<<Yeah, three questions>>
<<<We'll answer your questions three, Aaron Waters>>>

Sensing that these currently invisible creatures were in control and that they weren't going anywhere until he got his mind together, Aaron took a deep breath. He realized he was breathing in space and came up with his first question:

"How am I breathing right now?"

<<Easy, we project local atmosphere>>

<<<Like how you fart out of your human butt. Haha!>>>

Their voices were so familiar. He was reminded of a dream he'd had recently.

"How long have you been following me?"

<<Hmm, well, that one's a little bit more difficult>>

<<<Yeah, we don't do linear time, partner>>>

<<Ask another one, that one doesn't count>>

"Okay, why are you doing this?"

<<It's our assignment. It's very important to us that you stay on track and not have your brain scooped out by the Hunters for their neural network>>

<<<It is critical to our very existence, Aaron. We need you>>>

<<You're also the most convenient being to influence in this timeline. It's a very sacred role. You are, however, entirely not special>>

<<<As you suspected>>>

This timeline? Sounds pretty linear to me, Aaron thought. *Enough of this, I need to know what they are.*

"Just what are 'the Magi?'"

<<Awww>>

<<<We thought you wouldn't dare ask>>>

<<Alright, here we go>>

The two Magi appeared to him, illuminated without any light shining upon them. They appeared to Aaron to be human babies with enlarged foreheads and some strange technology orbiting them. The odd machines that surrounded these space babies also delved within them and then outside of them again. They seemed to dance with energy. Their eyes were closed but they were grinning through barely parted lips. The light radiating from them matched a tinny sound, almost musical, which emanated from the aura surrounding them. He recognized it as the bells he'd assumed until this point were his own private psychiatric malady. The two beings interacted in a way that suggested they were communicating at a rapid rate. There was, Aaron observed astutely, something going on here. He noticed they didn't have any navels. Indeed, there wasn't a single belly button between the two entities.

<<<The Magi are a cluster of clonal clowns>>>

<<We also alliterate a lot>>

<<<We can alter space and time to suit our needs>>>

<<The entire material universe is to us like clay is to you>>

<<<We don't need food>>>

<<Our food is in the Cycle>>

<<<The Cycle provides>>>

<<Providence is in our nature>>

<<<Our only mission is to ensure our creation>>>

<<We exist prior to our inception>>

<<<When that moment arrives>>>

<<We cease>>

<<<It's the Pernicious Cycle>>>

Aaron blinked and they were gone. *Where'd they go?* He began to panic and breathed consciously for a moment. The mischievous, machined cherubim had entirely dematerialized again. *Have I found myself caught in some heavenly jape?* he wondered. Aaron figured it must take a great act of will for them to physically appear. All around him the empty vacuum of space expanded outwards, dizzying itself in his mind. The Magi were no doubt keeping him alive with a false atmosphere. Their technology still hummed in a slight jingle, like chimes ringing under water.

<<<Pretty cool, huh?>>>

"Yeah, pretty cool, guys. Holy smokes," Aaron said.

<<So where do you wanna go?>>

"I think I want to go back and meet Gloria for our date," he told them.

<<<Poor sucker>>>

<<He has no idea she's a snake>>

<<<Or that he's already half a week late for that date>>>

<<Look, Aaron. We can go back to Earth, but it's going to be next week there since our mode of travel folds space-time>>

<<<Are you sure you don't want to go back to Earth and witness neo-Amazons slaughter a mastodon?>>>

<<We can go anywhere in the universe and he wants to go home>>

<<<Typical fun-hating human request>>>

Aaron could feel the vast loneliness of the space between stars. The intonations of these invisible time-bending cyborg-baby cosmonauts echoed through his empty head. He knew he was stuck with them and perhaps he had *been* stuck with them, but he didn't know for how long in either direction. *Maybe they'd always been there and always would be.* Somehow, he felt he'd been cheated. *But then, how many people had been jettisoned off of Earth and killed in a trap by intergalactic human hunters? And how many people had been protected by time-traveling cyber babies?* Aaron admitted to himself he just didn't know. He should've used his questions better. It made him feel worse, wasting his three questions. Before this, he could blame his awful circumstances on the greed of the rich or his own ineptitude.

Aaron had been raised in one of the traveling slums they called FEMA camps but he had at least gotten a standard VR high school education. He'd spent a year attending college before loans were no longer extended to him and the only thing he'd gained was a cynical Marxist chip on his shoulder. This aegis of communist ideology had formed a shield made of irony which had briefly protected his mind from the crushing reality of carbon-based ecological capitalism. He had survived in low-paying jobs with no hope for a future because there was no future he could imagine. Life on Earth had been one rolling disaster.

In his current emergency, Aaron had to look inward. The entire galaxy provided a silence and a mirror for him to do this. As he did so, the Magi no longer giggled in his ears. The sound of their angelic machinery rang only faintly, hardly above the tinnitus he'd acquired from running heavy equipment the last two years. Nothing made sense anymore. He began to think about

<<Suicide isn't an option, Aaron>>
<<<Seriously, dude?>>>
<<Do we have to save your life *and* give it meaning? Unbelivable>>
<<<Sic pun, partner. Amazons, it is!>>>
<<Amazin'>>

ZAP!!

Aaron's whole spectrum of sensation seemed to warp and jerk. Something was changing, but he couldn't tell what. His field of vision rippled and folded. The sound of crackling cellophane whispered between his ears. Stars zippled by soundlessly and throughout the experience of these preternatural phenomena, he worried. What worried him was not where he was going, but about the currency he would need when he got there.

★   ★   ★

In a spaceship somewhere between Mars and Earth, the Pernicis were settling into their new dwelling. Mrs. Jennifer Pernici, the daughter of MonDow employee Jerry, the office manager, turned to her husband and said:

"Honey, I can feel the baby kick."

Dr. Raphael Pernici was a Ph.D., not an MD. But he knew he would probably have to deliver his wife's baby while aboard the spacecraft. It would be a first for human history. And yet whenever he began to get anxious, a strange melody of soothing silver bells chimed merrily in between his ears. It seemed to suggest:

<Everything will be just fine...>

He felt his wife's belly move under his fingertips and smiled warmly.

CHAPTER 13

Buy me a drink, sing me a song,
Take me as I come 'cause I can't stay long.

–Tom Petty and the Heartbreakers,
Last Dance with Mary Jane

It was happy hour at the Wiggle Room in downtown Tampa and the young professionals were starting to filter in. Harold Wong, Doctor of Feng Shui, had begun to reluctantly commingle after ordering a Cuba libre from the bar. He decided that he might dance tonight and maybe even perform karaoke if some kind stranger bought him a second or third drink. He had already forgotten that he was trying to forget something: the massive sinkhole from earlier in the day.

"So how was your day? What did you say you do, again?" a leather-skinned bleach blonde Florida barfly slurred at him, booze blind.

And that's when he remembered what he was forgetting and his mood soured a bit.

"My day? It was... exciting," Hal Wong lied to her.

"Exciting?! Well, that's gooood!" she replied naively.

"A little too exciting for my taste. You will excuse me," he said as he casually removed himself while taking a sip of his drink.

"See ya, honey!" she said as she rolled her eyes almost audibly.

The crowd seemed to envelop him. The room's laughter and excess began to offend him. He could no longer ignore the work he had to do. Hal changed his mind and decided to leave the establishment. But before he could step out, something caught his ear and he instinctually started eavesdropping:

"Yeah, it was crazy, apparently the ground just opened up and swallowed him. No trace at all, he's now hundreds of feet underground, or underwater, or whatever is down there."

"It's such a shame, he'd just been promoted to Media Specialist II."

"Are you guys talking about the sinkhole in the fiber fields today?" Hal interjected with a buzz.

"Yeah man, our buddy was lost today," one of the two sullen men answered.

"I'm real sorry to hear that. I was there today: I tried to warn everyone. But hardly anyone listened," Hal told them.

"What d'you mean 'you tried to warn them'? How the hell would you know beforehand that a deadly sinkhole was about to open up?" one of the men asked with a tinge of anger.

"How much and of what quality is the time you have currently?" he asked them in reply.

The two men facing Dr. Wong looked at one another and back at him. The geomancer looked to his left and right, then pulled a small weathered notebook from his back pocket. The notebook was embossed with a small yin yang surrounded by Chinese symbols and sealed with a purple ribbon.

"Gentlemen, this is my tome of divination. I created it when I graduated from discipleship from the last master of the form of feng shui known as Flying Star. It contains all the charts that with the correct knowledge one can comprehend current, past, and future events."

"Dude, do you make a living doing this?"

"Yes, although I have a couple unpaid interns helping me. Mostly what pays is the analysis of construction plans for Chinese real estate developers."

The two dudes looked at each other again and laughed. They retained open smiles and sparkling eyes. They had forgotten their grief and were in awe of the lucky little man sitting across from them, pointing to his magic charts.

"Anyway... as I was saying, this is my journal. I can input any situation and discover the nature of what will occur. On this day, death and disaster was divined by the time and place of the meeting site and by other details," the geomancer said vaguely and took a draught of his beverage.

The dudes looked at each other again and tried to form a question for the man who they now regarded as a sort of Asian leprechaun.

He continued, "that sinkhole was predictable to some degree. Technically speaking, in regards to the press meeting that occurred before the disaster, my charts signaled to me the untimely stars of the element of Earth numbered two and five. Being that we were in a part of Florida that has drained its aquifers almost completely in the past century and being that group of people and our equipment were ourselves a significant mass upon the land, it was easy for me to see that the ground could be giving out long before I felt the first rumble."

"That's too much, man. I can't believe it," the one guy said to the other.

"I just wish some of them would've listened," the other said.

"Some did listen and stepped a few feet away from the epicenter of the sinkhole. But for many, it was too little too late. And now my friends, I must bid you a good evening and go dance," the fortuitous one said to his new friends as he handed them his business card.

"Wait! Let us buy you a drink!"

★   ★   ★

At the very same time that his new buddies were ordering Dr. Wong a second drink, the bureaucrat known as Rand Fornhinder was stewing about his office in Tampa.

Fornhinder had forced his employees to stay late as misplaced retribution for his embarrassment at the hands of Freedom Vinolte and Dr. Wong earlier in the day. He'd barely escaped from the sinkhole with his hide intact and the mortal terror and resultant humility inflicted upon him had only made him all the more determined to unearth the corruption of government workers everywhere.

"Ruby Schofield," he called through the phone intercom on his desk.

"Yes, Mr. Fornhinder?" she responded alertly.

"I told you a million times: call me Rand. It saves time. Anyway, come to my office." he told her testily.

Ruby Schofield was a gorgeous yuppie princess. She had fire-red hair, green eyes, and espresso-colored skin with chocolate freckles. She was the sort of human that could only exist in that particular century of America. Her administrative talent and unique beauty were entirely wasted in the tragically incapable office of Rand Fornhinder's Bureau of Efficiency in Government.

"'Ruby Scho','" the rotund old bureaucrat seemed to almost scoff as his employee entered his office.

"Yes?" she responded with grace.

Her entire presence resonated with reception. She was ready to take detailed instructions and execute.

"Your name came up today. You are coming up in the search results of scientists performing studies. There is some sort of, uh, proteins, which plants produce which are also called 'Ruby Scho.' Some of these studies are funded with federal funds. I believe that this wastes their time and our tax monies. You must tell people who call you Scho' not to do that anymore. Anyone who refers to you must henceforth pronounce your entire surname. This is not debatable."

She looked at him and felt deep, abiding disappointment. Her throat ached with the anger she could not release. The wrongness of having to stay late for this swollen appendix of a person washed over her and she could feel her rage develop. She wasn't an angry person but she found this visceral feeling overwhelming her. Her hands clenched and her body willed itself to strangle her boss but she bit her cheek instead, sweat beading on her forehead.

"Is that all, sir?" she forced the words out.

"Yes, you may go," Rand Fornhinder dismissed her from his bloated presence.

Back at her desk, Ruby fumed briefly. *If he wants me to stop being Scho', he'll have to pay me more.* Many vitriolic substances release fumes when agitated, but Ruby turned her attention to the task of comprehension. She would not be telling people they couldn't call her Scho' anymore. Instead, she performed a brief search that yielded Rubisco, which she vaguely remembered from her undergraduate days as a biology major. She sat there and sifted through scientific studies and articles, all of which she was able to gain access to with her fortuitously unexpired university email address. She didn't find anything particularly interesting or which she was not previously aware of. She did notice that a lot of the studies had been undertaken by a company called Monsanto and released by Freedom of Information Act requests. Then the Monsanto articles stopped abruptly. There had been dozens of studies a year and then nothing. So Scho looked up Monsanto, it turned out to be an old biotech and agrochem company. It had gotten bought out by Dow Chemical which then formed the giant conglomerate MonDow. And that's when her research got interesting, the year that the buy-out happened was the same year that the studies dried up. And there were no further Rubisco studies from MonDow, at least none that she could see. But she saw that within a year of the merger,

MonDow's revenue was way up. And in the few years that had since passed, the stock price had more than tripled. It was a coincidence that she couldn't just accept. *How could a company that had been so prolific at studying this protein suddenly give up when they got acquired? And why would the valuation of the company go up so much?*

She decided to submit a FOIA request to unearth any study that MonDow had performed with federal funds. In the meantime, she moved to understand what had occurred to secure that company such an increased market cap. What she found almost caused her to lose her peace. She saw that the merger also corresponded with the rise of the fiberweed and the creation of the new Department of Permaculture. This moment also coincided with MonDow sale of the fiberweed's growth-inhibiting enzymes.

Scanning over the results on her screen she overheard her colleagues talking in hushed, panicked tones and she looked at them over her shoulder. She was suddenly paranoid. The Department of Permaculture was the one government agency they were not supposed to mess with. Fornhinder had told them to ignore their inefficiencies because they were a net positive to the budget. Ruby knew their business was fiberweed management and ethanol production, both of which were politically non-partisan. If Rand or any of Ruby's colleagues saw her investigating fiber-related business, they would have stopped her in her tracks and probably tried to get her canned.

What's going on here? Ruby Scho' asked herself, feeling suddenly alone in an ocean of intrigue and danger. She had a feeling this mystery could have the power to transform her world.

"Hey Scho'!"

Ruby jumped out of her skin and swiveled from her computer's holographic projection of scientific studies and news stories, which fluttered from the air like leaves of paper and vanished upon the ground.

"Jeez! You scared me," she said with a hand over her heart.

"Oh, sorry. Hey a bunch of us are going out for drinks once old Fart-hider lets us out if you want to join us," her colleague casually mentioned.

"I'd love to, I just have a ton of stuff to do here. Another time," Ruby told him, trying to look innocent and buried in work.

"Ruby Schofield," Fornhinder's voice came through the intercom.

"This sucks. I hope he doesn't keep us here much longer," the colleague whined.

Ruby pressed the button to connect with her boss, "Yeah, Mr. Fornhi-, I mean, Rand?"

"Come into my office, immediately."

She always hated going to his office, but now she kept getting called there and it was after hours so she felt extra frustration. Usually, the main problem was that Rand Fornhinder's office smelled of stale farts and his cheap aftershave. She felt she had no choice but to get up and make the trip down the hall. When she got up, she looked around and no one in the office was working on anything. They were all grouped up together and chatting. Everyone was just trying to while away the moments before the boss let them leave. They were being inefficient.

"Miss Schofield," Rand addressed her to Ruby's mounting disgust.

"It occurs to me that I wasn't clear with you here before and that I may need to appeal more to your, ah, youthful exuberance. I want to make working here, ah, appealing to you. So, after some thought, I'm going to try to relate to you,"

Oh God, please don't. I wish he wouldn't. What did I do to make him want to say this?

"You see, I've been following this economist who says we need to engage more with the young workers in the workforce. Now, as you know, I have been formally retired for some time. And, I'll remind you, that although I technically make more money than you in this position, I do donate all of it to our city government to help them with their bottom line. And so, as a result, I live off my meager investment returns, social security, and my pension from my previous position as deputy commissioner for the Public Works Department of the City of Tampa, which I held for the maximum time," Rand gloated.

Ruby wondered why he would even bother. She truly didn't want to relate to him as a person. He was the direct source of the lion's share of unpleasantness that her occupation forced her to endure. She saw him as the embodiment of everything that held her down in the world: the old way of doing things, the old way of understanding how things work in the world, the old boys club of money and power, and the various ways she could be excluded from benefitting from that whole arrangement. The more she thought about it, the more she despised him.

"Miss Schofield," he looked her up and down and licked his lips, cleared his throat, and wiped the sweat from his brow.

"What?" she fired back at him.

"Is there anything I can do to make your time here more, ah, enjoyable?"

Ruby knew he was a disgusting old man, and never suspected him of any malfeasance before, but wondered now if he was somehow trying to offer her career favors in return for personal intimacy. The thought was so revolting she lost her train of thought.

"I'm sorry, what?"

"I know that young people need to be, ah, they need, ah, a purpose, and to feel good about their role in the workforce. And as your superior I want you to know if there's anything else, anything at all, that I can do to make you happier. I would like you to just let me know. Okay?"

"Okay, thanks Mr. Fornhinder."

"Please Miss Schofield, call me Rand," he bubbled, feeling proud of his oration at her and forgetting he'd told her that a million times.

"Not unless you call me Scho'," she told him and walked out.

What a dirtbag. Is that what he'd been doing in there? Listening to economists talk about how to engage young workers? Is that why he's keeping us all here this late?

Ruby suppressed her anger and transformed it immediately, subversively, alchemically, telling her colleagues on the way back to her desk:

"Fart-hider says everyone can go. You're all done for the day."

"Hey! Finally! All right! You sure you don't want to come to the Wiggle Room with us? We're singing karaoke!"

"No, I have some work to take home with me. Next time," she promised.

By the time Mr. Fornhinder worked up a proper reply to Ruby, elaborating in his mind why he couldn't call her 'Scho' because he was in a position of authority but perhaps after work over drinks he could, since that would be technically outside of the working relationship; by the time he'd done those mental gymnastics and called her on the intercom, Scho was already dismounting her bike and locking it to a fence outside her apartment. And by the time he'd discovered there was no one else left in the office, she had ordered delivery, opened her tracer's holographic research app, and resumed her inquiry into MonDow and the fiberweed.

★   ★   ★

Simultaneously, similar abuses of power were amok across town.

"Hey, Dr. Horn. You wanted to see me?"

"Yes, nurse Day. C'mon in. Close the door," Dr. Eddy Horn told his nurse while seated at his solid oak desk.

"Gloria," he said, "have you made a date with that Mister..." he looked down at the file in front of him: "Mr. Waters?"

"Yeah," she responded.

"Good. If we can get him in here to sign some things, I think my grad students will be able to get us a whole lot of grant money for his novel psychological malady with the hallucinations and the manifestations. You think you can do that for us?"

"Probably not," she replied realistically.

"Well, I hope so. We need all the funds we can get. Lord knows we don't get much from the insurance companies anymore," Dr. Horn told her.

"I just hope he's not another one of your long-lost twins," she quipped and immediately regretted it.

"Nurse, you know we don't discuss things like that, certainly not so lightly. Get the man in here or you might be needing to find another job," he spat out shortly.

She left his office quickly, her skin flushed and burning with repentance. In truth, she didn't understand why a nobody named Aaron Waters was so special to Dr. Horn. He seemed like just another slouch injured on the job. She treated him the way she was trained to, with dignity and respect, and making him feel special, knowing full well she'd likely never have to see him again. But now Dr. Horn had told her to make an off-hours call to him and he was forcing her to go on a date with him and try to get him in for God only knows what sort of experiments. She hated having to do dirty work to get his grants. *Maybe working elsewhere wouldn't be so bad,* she told herself as she got back to her routines. But the sense that she was doing wrong wouldn't leave her. She felt bad for Aaron and felt remorseful that she was being coerced to attempt manipulation of his emotions.

Dr. Horn too was full of regret. Mostly he regretted drinking corn whiskey in the office and spilling the beans about his secret twins experiments to nurse Day in a moment of weakness. He never should've told her about it. It was formally on a need-to-know basis and a highly scandalous experiment to begin with. It was also an ongoing failure. He feared someday it would become a public embarrassment and he would have to give up the luxuries with which he had grown comfortable. He just hoped he would die first and not have to face the public scrutiny of his ethically bankrupt work. He had lost everything once by putting money his entire fortune on the stock market when it was booming and then bearing the full brunt of the bust. He'd bought high and sold low, and he wasn't ready to lose it all again.

Sitting in his office with the door locked, swilling whiskey, he reminisced about the secret study and its subjects: two sets of identical twins orphaned at birth. One pair was male, and one pair was female. The twins were then split up and reassigned. He'd had their birth certificates and social security cards changed to reflect their new names: Freedom and Marshall Vinolte, and Buck and Tricia D'Aster. They would never know their true names or that they had a twin. Freedom and Marshall would be raised as siblings in an opulent setting with disposable income and all that came with that: being taught by educational professionals instead of an educational computer program, access to the national parks and animal preserves, and given a wholesome diet. Buck and Tricia were to be raised in a (permanent) temporary disaster relief camp by a sterile couple representing the working poor.

The purpose of the study was to prove his thesis that it didn't matter where you came from, one could make their way in America regardless of their circumstances. Dr. Horn's thesis was to show that nature could beat nurture and that the American dream remained alive and well. But the outcome of the twins' lives thus far was inconclusive at best and antithetical at worst: while wealthy-at-birth Freedom had become immensely successful, her poor genetic twin sister had gone missing from a university research position. And while impoverished-at-youth Buck was finally making a decent living, Buck's richer twin brother had also disappeared after coming of age and traveling aimlessly around the country, broke and desperate for years. One of the twins from each sibling set was missing or otherwise unaccounted for, and one of each was doing well. The data gave no significant indication one way or another regarding economic opportunity in America. But the experiment could be blamed for the ruination of at least two lives, and the damage could never be undone.

The high cost and the dubious nature of the study made it a wash, but it remained a secret. At least until Ralph Burgman discovered a man who looked just like Buck D'Aster living in an illegal brush camp. That man, Marshall, who Buck would later learn was his twin brother separated at infancy, told Ralph he hadn't seen or heard from his sister Freedom after she kicked him out of living at her apartment. Ralph pulled Marshall out of the fiberweed that day and took him to HQ to show Buck. When he asked what his sister looked like, Marshall showed Buck a picture of what appeared to be his own sister Tricia and that's when he started to get the feeling something *really* weird was going on. Buck then spent much of his life savings on private medical examinations where they discovered radio chips and traced them back to a Dr. Eddy Horn. Buck would've made sure Dr. Horn paid for it one way or another, but once confronted the doctor ultimately reimbursed Buck for the exams and made Marshall whole enough to find a place to live and go back to school to learn a trade. Buck never had much to do with Tricia ever since she went off to college and he went to work in the Last Gasp logging effort, but he did wonder what happened to her when she went missing without a trace, and if it was in any way related to the Dr. Horn experiments.

To Dr. Horn, the rediscovery of Marshall Vinolte threw the logic of his ill-fated and ill-conceived study into even greater question. *How could a man like Marshall, who had been given all the opportunities of life end up homeless, while his identical twin Buck D'Aster, who had been starved of these opportunities, end up the successful one? And how could Tricia D'Aster, who had achieved above-average success in life, after enduring an impoverished childhood, just disappear one day? And what about her twin, the dynamo Freedom Vinolte?* In light of the other facts of the case, he found Freedom's stellar success all the stranger. He had expected the richer twins to succeed in life, naturally, but how had Freedom succeeded so very much while her adoptive brother had failed so spectacularly? *And why would Buck, out of all of them, end up thriving as well?* Eddy Horn would generally ruminate on these questions in a circular fashion while his nurses performed the actual work of tending to his patients.

…And now there was this Waters fellow to focus his toxic attention on.

★   ★   ★

While Ruby Schofield was continuing to look into the dark secrets of the MonDow Corporation and Dr. Horn kept reminiscing on his life's mistakes and scheming about future grant money, Freedom Vinolte was finishing up a strategic meeting of the minds.

"Are we all clear-headed and on the same page?" she projected to the boardroom on the top floor of MonDow's flagship building.

"Not really, Freedom. I'm at a loss here. We don't have any answers regarding the alleged Tree. Politically speaking it's an unmitigated disaster," Kevin Scalder, head of the Florida DoP, told her.

"I think I know what's going on, Freedom. You want us to brand the company in a new way to overshadow the Tree story," Jerry tried vaguely to placate her, a tactic that had worked for him many other times.

"Wrong, Jerry. That's the opposite of what I want you to do. By the way, have you heard from your daughter at all? I'm a bit more concerned about that criminal Dr. Pernici getting away with trying to kill me and stealing our rocket."

"No, unfortunately, Jenny hasn't called yet," Jerry told her.

"And Kevin, let's get you focused on increasing the fiber yields instead of worrying about the political stuff. Where's our representative for the Mars program?"

The people in the room all looked at one another. No one wanted to speak the truth.

"Well?"

"He resigned, Freedom," someone threw their voice from an unknown position.

"What!? You're telling me we launched a PR disaster to Mars and no one's managing it? For God's sake, when was someone going to tell me this?"

The room consumed itself in silence. Freedom sensed that her time was being wasted. Someone cracked each of their knuckles, one by one, underneath the solid black walnut table. It was Kevin Scalder.

"What the hell, Kevin? That was your guy, you told me he was solid," Freedom glared at him.

"Well, I was going to tell you, but the whole sinkhole thing happened. We were all really worried that you were alright."

"Don't be stupid, of course I was alright. We have contingency plans for a reason," she took a breath and a brief rest before speaking again. "I'm liquidating the media department, Jerry."

"What does that mean?"

"It means that you and all of your larval, coffee-suckling, screen-basking media techs are all fired," she told him coldly.

"Oh. Okay," he looked down at the table.

"Kevin, put all the funds coming from weed fuel into research and development of RuBisCO improvement."

"Freedom, you know that I can't just let you pull out all the--"

"*You* know that *I* know that you *can*," Freedom cut him off.

Everyone in the room turned to look at Kevin, who looked left, then right, and then his face flushed rosy. It was now abundantly clear to all present who *really* owned the Department of Permaculture.

"Here's what we're doing, people. We're going all in. I'm taking the reins, and we're going to ramp up the production of complex carbon. And we'll be essentially printing money. That's why I'm giving the fiberweed profits and the budget of the media department all over to Research and Development. The plan moving forward is to start producing sugar and protein with fibergrass in addition to the current ethanol output."

The room nodded in assent, hoping to avoid the wrath of Freedom.

But Freedom was lying. She knew what no one else in the room knew. The fiberweed already had an optimized version of the enzyme and she was partially responsible for putting it there. If the truth were ever to be discovered, she and MonDow would be ruined. If that happened, Freedom's worst fears would be realized – all the money she had made for herself and the shareholders would evaporate from her watersheds and precipitate into a handful of law firms' coffers for litigation fees. She would have to work tirelessly to position herself ahead of any potentially embarrassing outcome. But regardless of her obfuscation in that board meeting and at the podium before the sinkhole, someone equally ambitious and capable as Freedom was already fiercely investigating.

★   ★   ★

Ruby Schofield was slurping spicy noodles in her tiny apartment, scientific articles and financial news holographically littering the space, her research orbiting her like dozens of thin rectangular moons of information. At home, she could feel free from the prying eyes of her co-workers and her disgusting boss at B.E.G. and at last get to work.

Her findings revealed that many things had been tried to increase crop yields and decrease the amount of fertilizer and labor that a farmer had to put into a field. Scho kept turning up papers written by scientists keen on foiling the rising tide of fiber weed. 'Common bacterium modified to produce fibergrass pathogenicity,' promised one paper by D'Aster et al. She skimmed it. Ruby found that they had genetically modified a bacterium found in soil in order to try to reverse the weed's advance. She was fascinated now to be on the trail of this record of Science's attempt to deal with the fiberweed. It was so much different than the boring statistical research that Fornhinder had her working on regarding worker productivity and bad management.

Another paper by D'Aster et al. referenced a previous study by Ingham et al that just one GM bacterium of Klebsiella planticola could prove universally fatal to all plant life on the planet. The Ingham study, which had been carried out a little more than a century earlier, showed that through a simple twist of fate, the genetically modified bacteria had been contained and no damage was done. Ingham and others had thought that the modified bacteria could use byproducts from grain harvests to produce alcohol for fuel and to fertilize the soil. However, in the field, it was shown that the bacteria, which coated the root systems of crops, produced entirely too much ethanol and killed the next year's rotation. Ruby noted that D'Aster commented in the footnotes of her own study:

"It is an unfortunate turn of fate that we must consider the use of this option, but it may prove efficacious. The modified K. planticola produced by Ingham et al could be deployed to destroy the advancing fiber grass and incidentally, all our forests and other terrestrial plant life lacking the K. planticola resistance gene, as long as the destruction of the fiber is total. The trees and plants could then be replanted from seed banks."

The study by D'Aster et al presented an Arabidopsis thaliana strain of plant that contained resistance to the modified K. planticola bacterium. Ruby swooned when D'Aster mused that should the virulent K. planticola be released, there would be a contender to take over the plant kingdom. An epic battle between the giant grass and a tiny white flower would overtake the entire globe.

Her imagination was getting away from her but she steered it to the matter at hand. The paper concluded with D'Aster elaborating on the danger of this resistance technology falling into the wrong hands. The resistance gene would spell disaster if it were released because there would be nothing else to halt the tide of the weed. Luckily, she noted, it was a proprietary strain and had become the private property of the Monsanto Company.

Ruby looked at the year that paper was written. Ten years ago, ancient history. *What had happened since then?* She looked up Tricia D'Aster through the scientific article search engine. All of her articles were published between 7 and 10 years ago. There was a burst of productivity and then nothing. Ruby did a general search of the name 'Tricia D'Aster,' and saw she'd gone missing at the same time her articles stopped coming out. *Well, that makes sense,* she reasoned, *you can't write an article if you're missing.*

With this news, she figured that she'd reached an impasse in her research. She'd long since finished her noodles and gulped down the cold broth. Yet she felt a thirst: a thirst for knowledge, for camaraderie, and for something alcoholic. She thought she likely couldn't get all three in the same place, but she was doomed to try. Ruby decisively powered down her tracer and her accreted queue of holographic papers dissolved quickly into the ether. She was going out. She would be going to the Wiggle Room after all.

CHAPTER 14

My name? It's Odysseus, son of Laertes.
Known the world over for every craft and wile,
my fame unto heaven reaches.

Ruby Schofield slipped through the parted doors to the entrance of the Wiggle Room like dawn's rosy fingers. Though Dr. Harold Wong didn't make particular note of her arrival amidst the establishment's traffic, he did sense a change in the color of the room. And despite his partial inebriation and the fact he was on stage performing karaoke, his second mind was nevertheless busily tracing the source of the mood shift.

Scho' could feel the heat of the gaze of single men. She was waiting to get a bartender's attention as she glanced around the room, and like so many whacked moles, the men quickly took their eyes off her. Seeing them look away she felt self-conscious, realizing once again that to them her body was a commodity, her gorgeous presence distracting the men from their conversations. On the opposite of the equation, she could feel that the scarce women in the building immediately viewed her as a potential threat. Her pale cheeks flushed madder lake. She knew she had to find a sanctuary in that place and wondered why she'd even come. The flaming ringlets down her back danced while she nervously shook her head to tame her bangs. She felt trapped and alone in the crowd. It was torture; she was burning alive under the scrutiny of unscrupulous oculi, and her forehead began to glisten.

"Miss? Something I can get you?"

A hipster bartender's apprentice with golden beads weighting his thin, parted beard curlicues was offering Ruby his services.

"Dark and stormy. Please," she added.

"Coming right up!"

An eternity later the drink slid towards her on a paper receipt. She reached into her purse to retrieve some cash. The slip demanded 80 carbon. She put down five 20-gram carbon tokens and left the bar's vista. The bartender's apprentice snatched up her tokens and quickly lit them up on the illumination station to check if they were just charcoal fakes. Counterfeit carbon would always be a problem in America, they were told.

Ruby took the drink and looked for someplace dimly lit to hide. No such unoccupied refuge was forthcoming and to make matters worse an unfamiliar man in a hideous emerald suit had locked eyes with her in a headlong approach. Reluctantly she would have to engage him, however meeting this man would prove auspicious. The quiet, yet fortuitous nature of his presence dawned on her when he did not immediately address her. Instead, he seemed to attract her like a gravity field with an approachable gesture of affinity. The man had simply raised his left hand, offering his company like a fortune cat. She thought she heard him say "Hi," but it was too loud to be sure and his lips didn't even move. Ruby had considered evading the man with a deception. It would've been clean and easy, as the gesture left her ample time and space to deflect him. She could simply relay that she was meeting friends, but then she would have to spend the rest of the night maintaining an untruth, or else hastily imbibe her expensive beverage and hit the road in an early departure despite having just gotten there. Instead, she watched as he walked toward a small couch on the dark side of the karaoke stage, a spot she hadn't seen before. And she decided to follow, sipping her drink then setting it down on a small glass table near the couch with slight ferment. The stranger in the shiny green suit smiled at her with his eyes closed; looking, she realized, like a grasshopper.

The first words they exchanged seemed to Ruby somewhat mundane: with regards to the temperature, the layout of the room, and the lighting. She wasn't one for small talk and took advantage of the first moment of silence to draw her tracer. Any lesser man would've been offended that she'd pulled out her phone, but Dr. Wong looked deeply at Ruby's facial features glowing pale blue from the light of the tracer. "What are you looking for?" he asked her directly.

"Oh, nothing. Just something for work," she said.

"I see. And what is your work?"

"I work at the Bureau of Efficiency in Government," she told him.

"Ah, okay. I heard a boring speech from a Rand Fornhinder from that very same department today. The speech was very boring indeed! Were you at today's event?"

She looked over at him and chuckled a little, took a sip of her drink, and looked back at her phone. Her glasses flared like an opal with the light from her tracer screen, and her pupils grew wide.

"I wasn't there, but I heard about it and I know how terrible he is," she related.

"Truly the most ironically inefficient man. And your entire office as a whole is somewhat redundant, not to offend you," he told her, realizing his lips were loosened from the hooch.

"It's fine. I know. Come to think of it, I hope I don't see anyone from work here. They invited me here earlier but I went straight home from work to investigate this MonDow stuff," she replied serendipitously.

"Oh, interesting! That was another thing that came up today," Dr. Wong told her. "The MonDow executive, Freedom Vinolte, mentioned a BoE employee. Ruby Scho. And something about the photosynthesis efficiency of a plant protein called Rubisco. I can't recall some of the details. Would you happen to know her?"

"I uh ... yeah, I know Ruby pretty well. I'm her," Ruby revealed with a glimmer of astonishment.

"No, I mean do you know Freedom? She gave what I found to be a very intriguing speech. I was sold on it. Rubisco! Good stuff," he declared, having finally forgotten the screams of innocent victims earlier in the day when a massive sinkhole opened underneath them.

She wasn't sure he understood that she was the subject of the speech, but it didn't matter and she was ambivalent anyhow.

"'Freedom?' Never heard of her," she told him honestly.

"Hang on, you've got to see this lady. I'll pull up a video," Dr. Wong suggested, reaching for his tracer.

Ruby put her phone down and took another sip, the ginger and rum warming her palate, throat, and belly. She could feel her mind start to be rekindled, though more by Dr. Wong's enthusiasm rather than by the liquor or ginger root, his eyes twinkling in the dim light of the club like stars ancient sailors relied upon to navigate many waters.

She looked up at the stage where someone she knew from work was already blind drunk and making a fool of himself. In a moment Dr. Wong had pulled up a clip of Freedom Vinolte giving a speech. She looked familiar to Ruby.

"Holy Shit. That's her!" she exclaimed in marvel at the screen.

She took the tracer from his hands to be sure. It was the spitting image of Tricia D'Aster, the researcher of fiber-grass ecology and molecular biology who she'd been digitally tracing earlier in the night. It was a huge lead, or it was a big coincidence. She knew that when she got home, she'd have to dig into the history of both MonDow and Freedom Vinolte. Ruby felt laser-focused and she had to retreat to her apartment. She resolved to make a quick exit. She'd already drained her drink, and none of her co-workers had spotted her so nothing was keeping her from leaving immediately.

"It was lovely to speak with you. Enlightening really. But I've got to go. My name's Ruby," she offered her name to the man.

"Ah, okay. It's been an enchantment to meet you, Ruby. Mine's Harold, or Hal. Take good care and remember," he told her earnestly as they shook hands, "that the keys to magic and science are observation and intention in equal measure, and the dread of something after death puzzles the will, and makes us rather bear the ills we have, than to flee to we know not what."

Dr. Wong sat wondering about the brief flame of Ruby's visit there with him in the Wiggle Room. His was a curiosity that could never be fully satisfied.

What a strange man, Scho thought to herself as she approached the front door of the Wiggle Room. *Something after death puzzles the will ... bear the ills we have or flee to we know not what...?* Regardless, Ruby walked away fulfilled, her trivalent thirst having been successfully slaked.

★   ★   ★

Elsewhere, Gloria Day waited around for Aaron to show up or call. She was waiting like a spider in her web. She caught up with stories on her tracer while she waited. Holographic characters ebbed and wove upon her lap as she sat on a bench by the bus stop. Usually, this was the bench where she would wait for the bus to come and take her to the medical complex where she worked. She'd never spent so much time there on the bench. Buses and their riders came and went. She'd been plucked out of her routine and forced to experience the bus stop through the eyes of the bench. After a few waves of riders waiting for the bus to ferry them down the line, finally, the last bus of the night approached the stop. There were no passengers ready and waiting to board except for Gloria, but the driver made eye contact with her and knew immediately that she wouldn't be boarding.

As the driver stepped on the accelerator an advertisement on the side of the bus caught her eye, and she watched as it went past. The advertisement was lit now that it was getting dark and Gloria could see that it was different from any of the other ads she'd seen lately. It was a new poster, and yet still one she might've seen before.

Pulsing blue and orange rays of color lead her eyes to the center of the ad. It was an advert for a new product of some kind. She couldn't tell from the ad just what it was for. All it said was: "It changes everything." The center of the ad showed what appeared to be a small crimson red stone with animated images emanating from it. Behind the stone, a woman appeared to be deep in thought. The woman looked familiar. She looked like Gloria, but healthier. It was the Gloria that she imagined would exist if she didn't have to go to work every day. There she saw the version of herself that lay dormant, and somehow this ad promised her that the red stone could potentiate all of the things she saw herself doing: biking, gardening, writing, cooking, falling in love.

With the sour smell of ethanol-powered bus fumes greeting her nose, Gloria read the bottom of the ad. The bus began to pick up velocity but she was sure it read: "The iStone™. It's here."

How stupid, Gloria thought: *that's never going anywhere. It even sounds dumb: "iStone™," how pretentious. No one is going to buy one of those.*

She realized she'd gotten skunked waiting for Aaron Waters at the bus stop and started making her way home. She phoned Dr. Horn on the way and he picked up his tracer. He was still at the office. She could tell because of the background noise.

"Hello? Gloria?"

"Hey."

"Hey, aren't you supposed to be meeting that guy? Why aren't you?" he asked.

She was so frustrated and yet indifferent that she could barely respond in words. She resented that Dr. Horn expected her to do his bidding but never compensated her for any of his little missions.

"Yeah. I don't know. He didn't show up," she muttered.

"Well, where is he?"

Again, she became unbearably perturbed. She held the tracer away from her ear and looked at it before responding.

"I don't know where he is. I just wanted to let you know," she said.

"Well, you've got to find him! You can't just --"

She hung up on him. She'd had enough of that, thinking to herself *he can pinch his pennies and not give me overtime for this obscene task, but I can no longer pretend to care.*

Her tracer pinged at her, but she ignored his page.

★   ★   ★

Dr. Horn clicked off his tracer in a tiff. He knew Ruby Schofield was ignoring him. It seemed he'd have to track down Mr. Waters himself. He fumbled around in his pocket and once again engaged his tracer, looking to hire someone. He typed in "private investigator" and dozens of profiles appeared. The cheapest one was still more than the rent he paid each month to lease his office space. He just couldn't stomach it. He went instead into his desk and pull out an encryption insert. The tracer was now rogue. He accessed the dark pages and searched "private investigator" but the only services that came up were explicitly for assassinations. He tried "investigations" and negated the search term 'assassination,' which gave a handful of results. One profile stood out for its low price and its unique offering: Bodyguard and Investigations. *Two-for-one!* He contacted the lister and was surprised when a woman answered.

"Hello?"

"Yes, I, uh ... found a listing for a bodyguard and investigator. Is the price negotiable?" Dr. Horn asked as he immediately started uningratiating himself.

"No," the grainy, soft voice replied.

An uncomfortable silence followed.

"Okay, well I need to find someone. I suppose time is of the essence... when can we arrange a meeting?"

"I can meet you right now," the proprietor obliged, her boyish voice worrying Dr. Horn.

"Okay, come to the Bayview Medical Center in Tampa, that's where my office is," he told her.

"I don't know, that sounds unprofessional. Why don't we meet at a bar or something?"

"Fine. Let's meet at the McDonald's on 50th street in an hour?"

"Alright."

*   *   *

Dr. Horn finished some paperwork and got into his car to leave the office. He considered blowing off the investigator/ bodyguard. He was loath to spend any money, especially when he already had so many people on his payroll. But he couldn't resign himself to having made no significant contribution to the world of science and he was sure that finding Aaron would bear academic fruit. Specifically, he had devised an experiment where he would scan Aaron Waters' brain and subject him to stress testing. He reasoned that if he could replicate the dissociative experience that produced the acorn, he could find the underlying cause of the event. Even if he didn't profit from the finding, he would at least be remembered for it.

Dr. Horn began to feel nervous as he pulled into the 50th street McDonald's. Even though he stopped there to pick up breakfast for himself every morning, he seldom stopped by in the evening. He parked and reluctantly exited his vehicle. He had poor night-vision and didn't trust the darkness. He made his way to the door and entered the building, ordered a small coffee, and took a booth in the corner. From there he tried to observe all the traffic of the restaurant. But it was pitch-black outside and he couldn't even see his car. He drove a Honda Squire, like Aaron's, but a couple of decades newer. It was still too cheap of a car for a doctor to be driving.

A cloaked figure walked into the restaurant. It was somehow obvious to the doctor that this was his investigator. He waited for her to get her order and then waved. As she approached, he realized just how very small she was. She threw the purple cloak in the booth and addressed the doctor:

"Sup?"

A wave of blonde hair swooped over her shoulder as she began to devour the fries she'd ordered.

"You are my investigator?"

"Not yet I'm not. You gotta pay me, dude!"

She shoveled french fries into her mouth and smiled while chewing. Her eyes were glassy and squinty, and she seemed delighted to be there.

"Of course," he said with a sigh.

"It's 500 a week. Cash only," she said, feeding her face more fries.

"And what do I get for my money?"

"You get my patent-pending body protector and investigation services. Didn't you read the ad? By the way, why is yer tracer encrypted? Ya know these aren't illegal services, right?"

"Interesting. I was not aware of the legality. I prefer to be discrete when it comes to these sorts of things," he said with a shrewd hand gesture. Then the doctor jerked his coffee to his lips and got too much at once, burning his tongue. He hid the pain.

"Yeah. Well, that particular encryption app yer using just calls attention to yerself. You might want to deactivate it if you've been up to anything, just a tip. No charge," she grinned and ate more fries.

"Okay. Got it. So, what else do you already know about me?"

"Nothing interesting. I know where you live and work, where you went to school, and how much money you lost in the last economic downturn. I don't care to dig too deep with potential clients. Just enough to make sure they're not creepy and that there are no conflicts of interest, y'know?"

Nothing interesting, he thought. *Perhaps not yet!*

"Anyway, my name's Jaina Shields. I've never been to college. I always liked to tinker and I learned how to code and build computers on my own. A few years ago, I built this little doodad," she told him and put a small, circular metal device on the table.

She pressed a conspicuous button on the device and it vibrated and whirred. The button turned a blue color and slowly emitted an expanding field of visible energy. The force field soon contained both of them.

"This is just a personal-sized one. I can also make them much bigger…"

Dr. Horn sat awestruck and speechless inside the blue field

"No one can see the field from the outside and no physical forces can enter the field unless they have a shield generator of the same frequency. So, in here, we're impervious to gunfire, stabbing. Even most sonic and laser weapons are useless against us. We are for the most part entirely inviolate," she remarked to him as if she were selling him a magazine subscription.

"I see. So are there others like it?" Dr. Horn said with interest.

"Only a few. A couple of years back I sold the blueprint to a foreign country for a small fortune. Originally, I offered it to the Defense Department but we couldn't make a deal," she confided.

"Incredible. You created this without any help," he asked.

"Yeah, totally without the help of the inventors of capacitors and lithium batteries and stuff," she snorted sarcastically and looked at her tracer.

I'm boring her, Dr. Horn realized.

"Well, so I think I'd like to purchase your services," he offered weakly.

"Great! For you, it's a grand in advance and five hundred a week thereafter," she said, almost finished with her fries.

"Okay. I'll wire you the one thousand and then set up a recurring payment --"

"You mean you didn't bring any cash?" she demanded, holding eye contact.

"I don't generally need cash for anything. I just don't like those carbon tokens jingling around in my clothes. But I could certainly get you some if you just wait here or, or else I could meet you later," Dr. Horn said.

"That's alright. I'll extend you a line of credit until the next time we meet. Ten percent interest per week on funds owed. Here, you can hold onto this for now," she told him and slid the shield emitter across the table.

"Thanks. I'm good for it," Dr. Horn said, fondling the metal piece in his pocket.

"I know," Jaina told him, "but just in case, swipe your credit card in my tracer."

"Oh okay, no problem," he said. "Oh! I almost forgot the investigation. I need you to find a man named Aaron Waters," he told her, as he fidgeted with his wallet and swiped his card clumsily.

"Why?" she asked, scrolling through her tracer.

"I just do," he told her stoically.

"Does this have anything to do with your twins experiments?" she asked in a brazen retort with a morsel leaving her mouth and depositing itself between them on the table.

Dr. Horn was taken aback. He didn't think anyone except his circle of confidants knew about his shadowy past.

"I don't know what you're talking about," he lied.

"I'm sure you don't. Whatever, I'll find him. Twenty-grand finder's fee plus interest if you don't have cash up front. I'll send you an update soon. Smell ya later!" she picked up and walked out.

She's got my number, he told himself. *I have no recourse; I don't even know her mailing address. My lawyer would flay me if he finds out about this. The twenty grand is what hurts the most.*

He felt for the metal object in his pocket. It felt light. He thought it couldn't possibly emit a shield to stop bullets or lasers. He feared that Jaina Shields, if that was even her real name, had scammed him and given him a children's toy. Dr.

Eddy Horn quickly checked the menu to make sure they weren't giving out portable projectors in happy meals.

'*Shields,*' he thought, bewildered. *That's definitely a made-up name.*

Dr. Horn gained a fleeting sense of sadness and accomplishment at the dual possibility of having perhaps been taken advantage of, or perhaps having a top-notch inventor and hacker on the case of his missing patient. He wouldn't finish his coffee, as he didn't usually drink coffee this late at night. He simply threw the half-full, half-empty cup in the trash and walked out the door into the dark.

The outdoor humidity seeped into his clothes, which pressed their weight noticeably upon his skin. His only care was getting to his car safely. To him, crossing a parking lot at night was like crossing the valley of the shadow of death, but poor Dr. Horn feared many evils. He feared destitution, paltriness, and impotency in particular. Disquieted and crippled by the dark, he nonetheless found the way to his car like an owl in daylight. He hadn't thought about using the shield at all to protect him in his short, terrifying journey across the night parking lot.

*   *   *

The next morning over at the Bureau of Efficiency in Government, there was a bevy of email messages sent for one Ruby Schofield. The emails seemed to multiply whenever her attention was turned elsewhere. If she checked her inbox throughout the day there were rarely even one or two unread messages, but when she checked first thing in the morning or just before going home in the evening there was always at least a dozen.

They were never anything important. As far as she could tell, her role was simply to pass the emails along to the next person in the ongoing chain of shirked responsibilities. To reply directly to a message was seen as rude, confrontational, and even aggressive. It was expected that a message would be relayed several times before being forgotten or buried. It wasn't unusual for the initial creator of an email message to reply as a third party to the thread of a chain they had themselves started days, weeks, or months earlier. This was almost always the case. In more than one instance, Ruby noted that the originator of an email thread inadvertently answered their own query, and could be quoted almost begging for their own email reply-alls to stop filling their inbox. The thread would continue regardless until all parties had been properly notified and heard from, often multiple times, before the thread could be forgotten – forgotten or buried.

This morning, however, Ruby Scho' had so far left her inbox entirely unchecked. She thought to herself: *the email game is for the bored and unengaged.* She felt she had acquired an incredible insight the night before from that intimate stranger – that walking paradox of a man, Dr. Wong. She'd gained an appreciation for the fact that she shared a name with the most abundant protein on Earth: "Rubisco." She'd never thought about it. The enzyme puts molecules of carbon dioxide together … What would *she* put together?

From that introduction, she'd also learned that the primary researcher of her namesake enzyme, Tricia D'Aster, was somehow a dead ringer for Freedom Vinolte, an executive at MonDow. *How could it be possible that a researcher of enhanced plant physiology goes missing, and simultaneously their doppelganger starts profiteering from genetically modified plant-based fuel extraction?* Scho' kept going over the facts again and again in her mind instead of her normal routine of keeping the appearance that she was working hard at her job.

It was a lead that just begged more questions. Scho' wanted answers. Using her B.E.G. employee credentials, she clandestinely accessed the directory of addresses and tracers and came up with Freedom's personal contact information. Once she'd already gotten the info, she wrestled briefly with the ethics of whether or not to use it. She couldn't resist.

"Hello?" the voice of Freedom rang in the ears of Ruby Scho', who almost hung up in surprise.

"Hi," she replied.

"Yeah? This is Freedom," the baroness of verdure spoke dully into the receiver

"Freedom? Do you know Tricia D'Aster?" Ruby Scho asked nervously, not knowing what to expect.

"I'm sorry, who is this?" Freedom laughed and couldn't help but admire the forwardness of her questioner.

"This is … Ruby Schofield at the Bureau of Efficiency," Ruby told her the truth after deliberating as to whether to lie.

"What? No way! *The* Ruby Scho!? I can't believe this. Ruby, I use your name in speeches all the time. What's going on?"

"Oh, not much, I guess. You can just call me 'Scho'.' … I'm doing some research and it looks like someone named

Tricia D'Aster – who looks just like you? – *disappeared* just before you took your position at MonDow," Ruby related to her in an accusatory tone.

"Has your research revealed I was an unwilling participant in a twins experiment yet? Tricia is my twin, but we were separated at birth. So no, I never knew her. It's pretty weird. I don't like talking about it to strangers on the phone," Freedom shot back.

"It *too* weird, Freedom. You were in the same industry, studying the same things, and she was starting to threaten the claims that MonDow was just beginning to stake," Ruby replied, holding her ground.

"Ruby Scho' ... Darling, my life has been a series of impossible coincidences that have always turned out in my favor. I don't know what to tell you about Miss D'Aster. She was the *good* one, how about that? Haha! I'll tell you what I *do* know: Dr. Eddy Horn put on the experiments to track how social class affects something or other. If anyone knows about Trish D'Aster, it's him," Freedom said with perfect charm.

Ruby didn't want to trust her, but Freedom was so effortlessly in control that she had no choice but to act like she believed Freedom's words. In her gut, she could sense Freedom was lying.

"I didn't know that," she said, responding too slowly.

"Yep ... Well, if there's nothing else, I'll get back to my work. Let me know if you find anything interesting, Ruby Scho'."

"OK, thanks Freedom. Bye."

Ruby Scho' settled back into her workstation to pry into where Freedom was born. There was no information in the system about her parents or her city of birth. Normally she would see a social security number or at least a birthday, but here Ruby found nothing. There was nowhere else to look for clues: she would have to confront Dr. Eddy Horn.

CHAPTER 15

I don't know but I been told,
It's hard to run with the weight of gold.
Other hand I've heard it said,
It's just as hard with the weight of lead.

—**The Grateful Dead,** *New Speedway Boogie*

Somewhere east of Orlando a man changed the radio station in his truck.

This is NPR news: I'm Faarnz Qualifacker. Is the clandestine launch of the Pernicis to Mars a matter of national security? What about planetary security? The two scientists have the resources for a crew of 25, which some say could allow them to survive until old age and even raise children there on Mars. There's been no word from them, NASA, or from the financial sponsors of the mission: MonDow. As the rest of the world is forced to wonder from afar, what will become of the outlaw Martian family?

Another station was beginning to cut out. Buck D'Aster had been driving for hours, just burning fuel. The Department of Permaculture had awarded him a free lifetime supply of fuel after his 25th year of employment. He aimed to make the most of it and drove most of the time he wasn't at the office. He'd drive asleep if he could.

Now he was approaching the Atlantic coast of Florida, where the heavy moon was rising. He liked to drive along the coast and watch the moon come up over the ocean. It reminded him of his childhood summers walking with his sister Tricia down past the canals and onto the beach. Together they'd watch the blood-orange sky change by the moment as the sun plunged into the Gulf. The radio cut back in:

> — all about the newest reality rendering device: the iStone™. The product gets its name from the Philosopher's Stone, a mystical substance thought by ancient alchemists to do everything from turn lead into gold and achieve immortality, to washing dishes and taking the kids to school. The iStone™ is available at most gas stations but the question remains: What Is It? It has also been blamed for the recent malfunction of driverless cars. One user, reportedly frustrated by the traffic when trying to leave a gas station, inadvertently caused the artificial intelligence in the iStone to somehow create a virus that infected all DVs, causing many accidents and leaving the DVO lane almost entirely clear for that one particular vehicle.

Buck chuckled to himself. He knew the world was headed to hell-in-a-hand-basket but he was enjoying the ride.

Another user claims they no longer have to fuel up their vehicle ever since they shoved an iStone™ directly into their gas tank. Gas stations may have to reconsider selling them! Now, another strange thing about this product: nobody knows who is producing them, or how. It is simply doing what the ads say they do: changing everything. The unknown manufacturer has not even filed for a patent. And yet they are disappearing from store shelves. At last look, the price for one on eBay was over two hundred thousand carbon, but who on Earth would part with something that can fulfill their every desire?

Buck didn't know what way to feel about that new contraption. If he could've gotten free fuel without working for the state for 25 years, he would've done that instead. But if everyone started doing that, he'd be out of work. ...*But just how the hell does the thing produce fuel?* The question irked Buck more than a dry shard of fiberweed in his sock. It would seem there would need to be enough energy in the iStone™ to propel a vehicle, unless it somehow drew energy from its environment or unless it was also a small fusion reactor. But then, how was it also able to write a complex virus that instantly wiped out an entire continent of driverless cars? *It didn't make any sense.* He decided to make a stop at the next gas station to get coffee and take his mind off the strangeness of the iStone™ story. The billboards said that it was the last gas station for a while. Buck drove towards it in silence for the next few minutes as fresh-cut fiberweed fields expanded before him. He could tell from the low dust levels and the smell of grass on the air that the season's second growth was coming up. The hunting season for giant would be opening soon.

Light from the next town glowed orange on the horizon under the hazy, dark sky. He could see the gas station coming for a minute because there was nothing out this way except fiberweed contracts. Buck approached the station reverently, like an eternal shrine. He pulled in slow, careful to ease his truck over the lip from the road onto the parking lot. He cut the wheel, jammed it in reverse, and cautiously backed into a fuel stall. He twisted the key in the ignition and the engine tumbled to zero revolutions per second. Buck sat there for a moment and did a little meditation. He breathed in deeply through his nose, catching the first whiff of ethanol.

He climbed down from the cab and slid his worn Department of Permaculture credit card into the pump. He pumped fiberfuel into his rig until it was full, kicked a mud heel off the wheel well, and opened the cab. He stood for a moment and considered getting in and riding off, but something called to him from the Mart. As he slinked to the front door, he knew he might have to get a coffee. And if he did, it could be an all-night drive. If he got a beer instead, he would drive another hour, get drowsy, and pull off and snooze in the cozy cab of his truck – the way he always did. He started to lean against the idea of a hot beverage and went to look at the cold ones. Maybe a beer would be good to him: they almost always were. But before he reached the cooler aisle, something caught his eye from a shelf.

In clear plastic packaging, a reddish-golden pill seemed to draw him into its orbit. It was the iStone™, the last on the shelf, packed like a novelty item. It made grand claims about its efficacy:

"Contains a cure for male pattern baldness!

Will shut up the neighbor's dog!

Fixes most makes and models of cars and trucks!"

He saw the price tag but couldn't believe it. He didn't know that they made price tags big enough to hold all those zeroes. Something about the product just looked illegitimate. It seemed packaged so cheaply that it couldn't possibly be worth a full two weeks' salary. Just the fact that it was so expensive and he found it on a gas station shelf gave Buck pause. In a rare lapse of character, Buck picked up the iStone™ and brought it to the register.

"Evenin'," he addressed the cashier.

"Hey, how are ya? I see you got yourself the last iStone™! I hear they're about to be illegal. Something about the driverless cars situation? We just got them in on Monday. I hadn't heard anything about them. No one even told me they'd been ordered."

"I just heard about them on the radio. Said they can fuel a truck. I have a lifetime DoP card, but maybe it will come in handy. For this price it better," Buck told him.

"Well, I'm sure it'll fair dinkum pay for itself one way or another. I would've bought it meself if I had the carbon. By the way, is that your truck? I was lookin' at it during me smoko. Looks kinda funny. Have a nice night," the cashier said gratuitously.

"Thanks, you too," Buck said, thinking to himself *that cashier **sounded** kind of funny.*

He walked out to his truck and put the iStone™ in the passenger seat. Buck buckled up and drove off. He remembered he'd forgotten to get a beer, but he didn't care anymore. Just having the iStone™ in the seat next to him eased his mind. He could've driven all night up the Atlantic coast, watching the tide retreat from the old ghost towns and sunken cities, consumed by the waves one by one: Daytona Beach, St. Augustine, Jacksonville.

One night he filled up both tanks and all his fuel cans, got food provisions, and drove north until the sun rose, and still kept driving. He sipped beer all morning as he was the only one on the road north to nowhere. And as the sun rose, so too did the miles and miles of weed. In places, the fiber got so dense that it grew out into the road. It looked like no one was keeping up with it, but somehow the road appeared to still be frequented. Razor-sharp fiber-dust from the trampled GMO bamboo burned in his nostrils and tickled his throat. He didn't know how far he'd gone as the road signs were all becoming obscured with the second season mature fiber. As he continued to drive north, Buck noticed that the medians of the road were gradually shrinking and the road soon became one lane.

At first, he didn't notice the first leaf of fiber he drove through, but soon Buck was driving through so many fresh leaves that the noise couldn't be ignored. The sides of the road, which was down to less than one car-width, pitched up at 60-degree angles and fiber poured in all around him. Eventually, his truck's drive train got strangled with fiber. It took him 45 minutes of knife work to get his machine loose enough to reverse and turn himself around.

If a fiber stalk is allowed to live long enough to die of natural causes it simply falls over, leaves the dead husk, and from its carcass sprouts new ones. Without human intervention, the organism forms a giant interwoven mat. The mat can grow up to an inch per year, the fetid mulch helping the next generation fiber stalk to grow even faster and larger, and to root even deeper and stronger.

Buck was curious to see how far south the mat had traveled since that last foray into the fiber sea. But with a yawning surrender, he decided that it wasn't worth the risk and turned around. The sun was beginning to come up anyway. After a U-turn, he saw a billboard he'd never seen before. It read:

"Duval County Hopper Hatch: the most in a decade!

I wish the guys and me could get out here to hunt some giant grasshopper… that would be something, he thought to himself a mile down the road. He couldn't remember the last time he'd gone hunting. Had he ever been hunting at all?

The iStone™ glowed red in the passenger seat next to Buck. The red light filled the cab of the truck and Buck looked away from the road for a moment to see what was happening. The stone's light faded and it seemed to shrink back into its packaging.

Then Buck remembered: *of course we'll get to go hunting. Opening day is this weekend and we're meeting up out in the brush before dawn. They made the opening date sooner this year because of the high number of hatchlings.*

Seemed strange that he could forget something like that. He chalked it up to driving tired. He knew the road could play tricks on the mind. Buck looked down at the digital clock on the dashboard. He calculated the drive time it would take to reach his office. He looked forward to crawling into the cozy nap nook he had created under his desk and dozing off until the workday began.

CHAPTER 16

"The opposite of nature is impossible."

—Buckminster "Trim Tab" Fuller

The last thing Aaron Waters remembered was a flash of light. The moment before that he was floating head over heels in space and with him, the Magi had been singing a nauseating hymn about the space-time continuum. They had assured him he would pass out and forget the long journey, which he did.

He woke up in a breathable atmosphere with gravity comparable to Earth's. He was glad to have ground beneath him again, after floating around for who-knows how long. His interplanetary time-traveling companions had left or else become invisible again because he could no longer detect their jangly jibber jabber. He could feel a breeze all around him. The sun was on a horizon, either rising or setting. He was outdoors, maybe in the fibersea. The ground beneath his feet seemed to have no fiber: just dirt and miniature grass. There were no artificial lights anywhere.

Aaron picked himself up. He was clothed and he still had his tracer and his wallet. He dusted himself off and began to walk with clumsy steps through the lush grass. It was like the lawn of a wealthy person's home. He knew from previously holding a job as a landscaper that the fiber needed to be mowed to the ground twice weekly, or else it got stalky and rough. This grass was fine and springy, yet still longer than any lawn he could remember.

The light had faded, from which he learned that the sun was setting and not rising. A cool breeze whispered on his skin. He couldn't see any buildings around and he seemed to just be in an open field. He stumbled on, thinking this was not much different than trying to swim through space. He had been wandering for only a few minutes, just long enough to let his guard down. He started humming to himself. Suddenly there was a rustle ahead, but before Aaron could react, he was addressed:

"Halt! You are surrounded. Drop your weapons and you will be spared," a disembodied woman's voice ordered.

Shit, he thought, *I don't have any weapons to drop.*

He put his hands up and got on his knees.

"I don't have a weapon," he told them.

"We will see if you are lying," the voice responded.

Hands shoved him to the ground and patted his clothes. He was turned over and frisked harshly. They prodded his bum with the stock of a spear and looked in his mouth. Then they took his tracer and smashed it, and threw his wallet as far as they could. Various cards felt out midair and fluttered to the ground some 40 yards away. Aaron watched as his belongings were absorbed by twilight on the lush field.

"Stand up. You are our prisoner now. In the morning, the courts will decide your fate," the voice commanded.

Getting up on his knees he leaned over and picked up his broken tracer and put it in his pocket, feeling sheepish and violated.

He turned around with a jolt and Aaron saw the face of one of his captors. She'd blown an ember to light and given it to the rest of her party to light their torches. She was tall and blond, like Freedom but larger. These women were muscular and stocky. They were the largest women Aaron had ever seen. He was terrified.

"Guess our hunt has finished for the night. Let's move!"

Four of the giantesses moved up to walk in a formation ahead. He wondered if they were going to forget about him, but the fifth one waiting at the rear gave him a swift kick in the back to get him moving. Aaron glimpsed their finely crafted spears, swords, and shields. Ornate designs of copper, silver, and gold adorned their skimpy leather armor. One had a jewel-encrusted dagger on her thigh. He looked closely at her bow. It appeared to be constructed entirely of pure wood, and on the end of the arrow-shaft was the seamless joinery of a razor-sharp obsidian arrowhead. He stumbled along half walking, half running. He was about to open his mouth to speak when they began to converse.

"Ayla says she saw a herd of mastodons at Serpent's Tongue," one said.

"She probably just heard a couple of deer and got excited. She's not like Schala. Schala killed a gorgeous cave bear last night,"

"Schala killed a cave bear!? That lucky bitch,"

"Yeah, she said she's making its hide into a rug for her hearth."

"Hey! Where are we going?" Aaron tried to butt in.

His guard kicked him square in the tailbone and sent him to his hands and knees.

"Silly little piglet. He speaks to us like we are equals!"

"Speaking of mammoths, we need to set up a better trap than last season. Remember how the herd changed direction at the last second to avoid our net? I was thinking, we should put the net behind them and then..."

The Amazons continued to talk about hunting as they walked for an hour or more upon the lush grass. Finally, to Aaron's acute astonishment, the lawn yielded to a densely wooded forest of mixed conifers and hardwoods. The ancient sights and scents were ambrosia to him. He forgot he was a captive and took in the almost psychedelic atmosphere of the torch-lit woods. The moon was off in the distance, permitting a silvery haze to settle into the shadows cast by his captors' torches.

He had already decided not to speak anymore, but he wanted to ask questions. And looking out in every direction he saw endless Trees. *Once again,* he told himself, *just along for the ride.* But soon the intoxicating smells of woodsmoke and fresh, slow-roasted game penetrated his nostrils. Aaron was unendurably hungry and suddenly very tired. He'd never smelled fresh meat roasting over wood coals. The labmeat street food he was used to just didn't come close.

He thought back to his day: how his car was totaled, how he was almost swallowed up by a sinkhole, and then abducted by two different species of aliens outside of the Gummy Nugs© outlet, and now here he was at the mercy of these giant huntresses, their delicious wild meats roasting in the cool forest. Thinking it all over, he thought he had earned a hot meal.

Unfortunately for Aaron, his captors felt differently. He was unceremoniously lowered into a circular pit too wide and too deep for him to escape from. Down against the damp earth, he felt that he had no choice but to curl up and rest his weary head, and to try to stay warm as the giantesses celebrated above him. They tossed down a gourd of ice-cold water, and some scraps and bones from the feast made their way to the bottom of his pit as well.

Aaron woke up at dawn with an eschatonic fever-wave of panic as two more men had joined him in the pit over-night. One was in the middle of speaking to the other:

"I don't know why I let you convince me escaping was a good idea. There's nothing out here except beasts, trees, and huntresses. We'd be lucky if they let us live after this. Where were we going to go? We can't hunt or fish, and even if we could, we might only survive for a couple of months until they find us again," he said in a high pitch.

He didn't have much facial hair and spoke with a higher voice than Aaron had ever heard in a man. The other man sounded similarly boyish and Aaron thought perhaps these two were youths, but their baldness made him think they must be around middle-aged. He couldn't grasp why they were so pear-shaped, though.

"It's all in the spirit of adventure, my good companion. What have you ever done in your life besides work in the power plant? You have always done exactly what the hunt-resses wanted. It was time for us to live a little!"

"Well because of that, we won't be living much longer, I fear."

"Hey. Before we get into the specifics, may I ask 'Where are we?'" Aaron addressed them.

"HOLY COW! His voice is so low. He must be a seeder. Why would *you* want to escape?"

"Maybe this one grew tired of breeding huntresses all day. How dull," the other of the two man-boys responded.

"Breeding? I haven't been breeding at all. I was taken from a Gummy Nugs in St. Pete and then trapped in space or something, and now I've ended up here, wherever we are," Aaron replied

The two captives looked at one another and back at Aaron, then back at each other.

"He's a nut, absolutely mental...! Maybe that's why he escaped: they fucked him to insanity and he flew the coop!"

"No! They haven't fucked me at all yet."

"Not at all? That's unusual. Did you escape castration and live among us slaves with your seeds intact? Are you like us, an escapee?"

"No, I'm telling you I don't belong here. I was in Florida, USA. Tell me where we are!"

Aaron was getting frustrated and his captive comrades were beginning to notice. The two castratos inched away from Aaron in fear.

"He's crazy. The environment of the ancient empire of the USA was destroyed a long time ago. Everyone knows human life can't thrive there anymore."

"We should just ignore him."

Suddenly a gong sounded. One of the prisoners whispered to the other and they both looked up terrified. A rope was let down the side of the pit and expertly lassoed around Aaron's foot. They pulled him up out of the hole like a fish from the sea. At the rim of the slave pit, he was laid at the feet of a panel of three older huntresses. They began immediately to deliberate:

"This is an odd case indeed. Usually, this council is only called for disputes between huntresses. This one looks like someone's slave, but it doesn't have any identifying insignia to determine ownership. Therefore, we don't know where it came from. We are thus tempted to call you *our* slave, give you *our* insignia, castrate you and send you off to the nearest manufactory," the oldest of the three said, her gray hair looking almost purple.

"That doesn't sound right," he said after a pause.

"'Right?' You were found in a most peculiar place, with no provisions and no weapons. Our sisters were heading home from scouting for game. How did you just appear right there in the middle of the grazing meadows, several kilometers from anything at all; and without even a drop of water? And why have you come here?"

Aaron couldn't answer that: he didn't know where "here" was, and he hadn't truly "come" there so much as he was launched through space-time.

"I have come without a purpose, I guess you could say. I was freed from a cosmic hunter's trap high up in the stars and the next thing I knew I was here with you all," Aaron told them, wanting to sound believable.

"A trap? What kind of trap?" the youngest-looking Amazon asked.

"A trap for both men and women," he said.

"I should hope not. Men can be trapped quite easily, but to trap a woman is not a simple matter," the third Amazon retorted.

"In any case, where are you from?" the oldest asked.

"I'm from Tampa, Florida, USA," Aaron told them proudly.

He remembered his schooling and how everyone in the world was supposed to love America. Maybe this would garner him some leniency and they would let him go or send him home.

"Never heard of it," she lied.

"Sisters, what if this man came from beyond our walls?" the youngest asked the other two.

"That does seem likely. No brand? All the males must be branded and castrated, or else be registered as an XY. Sisters, look at his dark skin. I've never seen such a complexion!" the eldest replied.

"It means there's a problem. The shield may have failed somewhere. We should pay a visit to the nearest outpost. We can drop him off there," the third Amazon said, casting judgment.

"Hey? What is this place?" Aaron asked again.

"This is the Sisterland. Norwegia," the youngest told him.

But that's impossible, Aaron thought. "Wasn't Norwegia evacuated so forests could grow back and take carbon out of the atmosphere?" Aaron blurted out, reciting DAD's history lesson confidently.

"Hell no, stupid. Our foremothers would've never allowed that," another of the Amazons replied in insult.

"The force field is impermeable. We have our own atmosphere. No phase of matter enters or leaves the membrane. When the outer government decided to try and take responsibility for the carbon in Earth's atmosphere, we responded by making our own," the eldest explained.

"The Sisterland FOREVER!"

"FOREVER!" the three Amazons before him saluted and exhibited intense scowls of their fierce loyalty.

One of them even drew a jewel-encrusted silver dagger, which although appearing small in her hand was actually longer than Aaron's forearms.

Aaron felt uneasy. He was starting to get the idea that getting out of Norwegia was going to be much harder than just dropping out of the sky. And he still didn't know if he was even on the right planet. If he was indeed on Earth, had he traveled through time? He and his captors couldn't even agree on something as simple as the history of nations. Fortunately for his peace of mind, Aaron had gotten used to just going along with things. *How could the Magi have let all this crazy shit happen?* Somewhere or sometime (if those were the right words), he just knew those fidgety little scoundrels were laughing at him, perhaps composing long, pun-filled sagas about his unending misery, now amongst the giantesses of the Sisterland who were deliberating over whether to brand and castrate him.

★   ★   ★

Elsewhere, Buck D'Aster's workday was going smooth enough. He hadn't lifted a finger all day and managed to not be bothered very much in his office. All his attention was on going hunting this weekend. He had researched the lifecycle of the Giant Southern Grasshopper and purchased a carbon fiber crossbow that he'd found online. Instead of doing what the State of Florida paid him to do, he'd been planning the minute details of the hunting trip that he, Ralph Burgman, and a couple of guys from Burgman's crew would be undertaking. The idea for the trip had come up out of the blue. Buck couldn't recall who suggested it or when: all he knew was that they were going. Saturday morning loomed just a few dozen hours away, and in its gravitational pull floated daydreams through his head.

In one dream, a giant hopper leaps out from behind some fiber and over the hunting party. Buck shoots it in midair and it falls to the ground, kicking and foaming caustic cinnabar liquid from its mouthparts. Later they eat roasted hopper haunches and boiled fiberweed tubers around a small campfire made with dried fiberstalks burning ashy under the stars. In another, he stops one of Ralph's crewmembers from shooting a hopper because it is too small.

"We must conserve this resource for future generations," he piously explains.

And then a beast of a hopper catapults itself out of the brush, unseen until now, and flits its massive wings into a hovering flight. The gargantuan insect almost makes it out of range but Ralph arrows it with impeccable aim from 50 yards away. The hopper falls helplessly out of the air and cracks on the ground with a short thud, black blood spraying in the dust. Buck and Ralph make eye contact and nod in a manly way.

Buck snapped back to reality with a glance at his iStone™. He felt ashamed at how much he had spent on it. He'd spent much less on the crossbow and was probably going to get more use out of it. He didn't even know how to work the thing. He felt paranoid for a moment. Maybe that NPR radio show was a scam, somehow geolocated to sell him that one iStone™ at that precise moment. Could the world and its technology conspire so singularly against him? He didn't think it was possible. Aside from his tracer, how would NPR and the iStone™ people know his whereabouts. The timing seemed impossible. His phone rang and he picked it up.

"Hey Buck, it's Ralph. Hey, we're out here picking up where we left off after Aaron's little episode."

"Oh yeah? How you makin' out?"

"Well, started off great. But we're running into some dead zones. Looks fresh, but not anything I've seen before. Everything is wilting, but it's still green. Something killed it, something chemical or I don't even know what," he told him.

"Well, send me some pictures. I'll contact MonDow and see what they can do. Anyway, are we still on for this weekend? You and your boys got your permits and everything?"

"You know it, bud! Wouldn't miss it. Anyway, gotta run. Talk soon," Ralph said, signing off.

Dead zones? Buck hadn't heard that term since those Greenpeace freaks got caught releasing pathogenic bacteria into the fibersea. He remembered they had traced the development of the toxic genes back to the laboratory of his adoptive sister, Tricia D'Aster. He had been mortified, and probably passed up for a promotion because of it too. But that was before Marshall had been found and the eventual discovery they had both been part of Dr. Horn's secret experiments. And anyway, Tricia swore until she disappeared months later that she had nothing to do with the bacterium's release into the wild. But Buck always wondered about her after that...

And now he wondered if someone else had gotten ahold of and released the virulent fiber pathogen, or if the wild type was expressing the toxic gene mutation independently. He had involuntarily picked up more cellular biology than he knew what to do with. He knew it could be anything, and it would be weeks or months before they would get any results from the MonDow laboratory, which the Department of Permaculture was contractually required to defer to when such matters arose.

For a while, after his sister disappeared, Buck had been paranoid that MonDow or the DoP had kidnapped her to get the secrets of her anti-fiber research and shut it down. He knew how much money was at play and similar cases of scientists being sabotaged or murdered had been known to occur. But when his doppelganger turned up in a working fiber stand, Buck began to consider the world a more complex place than he could make sense of. The conspiracy theory that his sister had been kidnapped seemed closed-minded in comparison to the concrete fact that they had both been involved in an involuntary experiment involving his full-blooded twin brother. However, even with that knowledge, he could still not quite parse the fact that his sister looked exactly like Freedom Vinolte. *How could they be twins, too? How many more twins could there be? Did they all work in the fiber industry?*

Time seemed to be speeding up as he aged. The common pleasures he took for granted as a young man were getting rarer and rarer. And looking at the iStone™ on his desk he found that didn't understand technology anymore. He wished someone would explain to him what it was and how it worked. Then at that precise moment, the object began to glow in the periphery of his vision as a co-worker passed his office.

"Oh hey, Buck. You sprang for an iStone™! Wow, that must've cost you a fortune. Where'd you find it, on eBay?" his officemate commented, who also happened to be walking by at that strangely serendipitous moment.

"Nah, I got it at a gas station in north Florida. It wasn't cheap, though. What the hell is it, anyway?"

"Why —don't you know?" the man said, stopping and looking straight through Buck's skull into the wall behind him, "Why…it's a potential moment precipitator. It basically grants one wish, or something similar to that, a day. Why did you buy it if you didn't know what it was for? Oh well, regardless, what are you going to wish for today, Buck? Say, how about a free lunch for the whole office? Haha!"

"I wish for free lunches," Buck said, shaking the dull red sphere.

Nothing happened.

"Damn thing is useless," he commented, "how's it supposed to work anyway? It knows English and makes wishes happen? What is it, a genie in a bottle from the future? And you only get one a day? What if I wish for a million iStones, would I get a million wishes per day? What a stupid idea for a piece of technology. It sounds like a cop-out, or a Mac-Guffin to solve plot problems in some crackpot's first sci-fi novel," Buck told his coworker with frustration and tossed the object in his desk.

★   ★   ★

Meanwhile, Ruby Scho' was spacing out at her desk at work. Her radio babbled just below her level of awareness. Her mind was trying to work out what happened to Tricia D'Aster:

> *Did Tricia kill Freedom Vinolte and take her place? Did Freedom kill Tricia to steal her research and destroy her lab? Are they both still alive and playing the same person but always in different places in order to accomplish twice as much? Is it all just a coincidence? Am I crazy? Her thoughts were turning like a water wheel. The radio emitted a familiar jingle and it interrupted her train of thought. She listened,*
>
> *This is NPR News, I'm Startleby Juntaquiver.*
>
> *New projections predict the Martian Pernici family could survive for generations and perhaps indefinitely if they*

inbreed and incorporate the theoretical transhumanist technology that is on board their spacecraft. Some think they could produce a new race of Martian proto-human-oids, though scientists are saying it will take at least 10,000 generations and it is extremely unlikely they will survive even for a year.

In other news, the iStone™ is facing a total recall after the House and Senate rushed legislation outlawing such devices. The US Federal Government now considers these moment precipitators weapons of mass destruction, after the discovery that everyone forgot to flush the toilet yesterday morning due to the wish of an unscrupulous abuser of an iStone. Faarnz Qualifacker has more:

"Most of the lucky consumers who were able to buy an iStone used them to get free lunches for their office or to win the local lottery. We're told that so many people have won the lottery since the iStone™ came out that the total winnings divided evenly wouldn't even pay for one iStone. And yesterday, someone wished that every person in the United States would forget to flush the toilet today — and the backlash from this prank is only just beginning to be felt. After being confronted by the sight and smell of their own excrement, members of the Congress and the House moved swiftly, and legislation banning the devices has been voted into law faster than anyone thought possible. And now, barely 24 hours since the collectively flushless-morning, the iStone™ has been officially outlawed. Federal regulators are now

*tasked with getting all of the thousands of devices out of
the hands of the general public and into the care of the
Defense Department, as all across the country today not
one toilet was flushed..."*

Huh? So, they don't like the smell of their shit, Ruby thought.
*I hope they don't go after the TimeRend™ next. I can't stand to be
conscious through even one more of Fornhinder's daily meetings. If it
gets outlawed, I will literally die.*

She looked at the well-used TimeRend™ on her desk
and wondered about all of the times she fast-forwarded
through her life – all that lost time in the place of life experi-
ences that she had deemed not worthy of being remembered
or even experienced at all… *Where does all the Rendered™
time go?* Ruby Scho wondered.

Her desk phone beeped. She picked it up.

"Ruby, I need you to look into this iStone business. Call
up the FDA and find out how much time they are going to
spend gathering these iStones," her boss Fornhinder commanded her through the phone. "And find out how many
iStones they have. Maybe they can use them to wish the
others out of existence. Isn't that how they work? Look into
it and we'll go from there and circle back when you do.
Also, find out if we know how much it is going to cost if we
switch to the no-name brand coffee creamer. I want to start
saving more money around here. As you know…"

He continued to speak, but she instinctually went back
to spacing out. She'd learned long ago that once he'd said:

"As you know," that nothing else important or memorable was going to come out of Mr. Fornhinder's mouth.

Ruby thought to herself, pleased:

I don't even need to use my TimeRend™.

She put the phone receiver on the desk and allowed him to speak to the desk's surface while she reclined in her seat and wondered about the Freedom/Tricia mystery and the inbreeding transhuman Martians of the future.

CHAPTER 17

She's well acquainted with the touch of the velvet hand,
like a lizard on a windowpane.

— **The Beatles,** *Happiness is a Warm Gun*

D r. Horn hadn't heard from the investigator he'd hired
and it'd been way too long since their meeting. 'Jaina
Shields' had seemed like an alias even at the time of their
meeting and young entrepreneurs had scammed him before
once or twice: three times, max. Thus, when she called him
at his desk one day during lunch, she already had him at a
disadvantage.

"Doc, I think I've found Aaron Waters."

"You did? Thank goodness! That's wonderful, I was
beginning to—"

"But it's going to be difficult to rescue him," she told
him. "Expensive, too."

"Rescue?"

He didn't like how this was turning out. It sounded like
a big fat scam. It was something he might fall for at 4:30 on
a Friday, after a couple of (what he thought were) his secret
whiskeys (but every one of his staff knew).

"I don't know, it sounds fishy. Where did you find
him?"

"He's been laboring in a Norweg power plant," she told
him bluntly.

"Norweg? Like *Norwegia,* Norweg? I didn't think they let anyone go there," he said with genuine surprise.

Dr. Horn swore he could hear Jaina roll her eyes during her furtive silence. He reasoned that the story she'd just told him must be either a great lie or the unlikely truth. He reached for the whiskey he had stashed in the bottom drawer and poured a double.

"I dunno really how he got there, but I think he's being held prisoner. Anyway, if ya want me to get him it's going to cost a fortune. The carbon credits fer the airfare just to travel there and back are going to be outrageous. And the highly hazardous work environment too is what's expensive fer you to compensate me properly. So, yeah..."

Truthfully Edward Horn had placed his last hope of a legacy on the shoddy chance that there was an undiscovered medical condition, or parapsychological malady, or perhaps a metaphysical conundrum hiding between the ears of the acorn-bearer Aaron Waters. Dr. Horn began to think he'd trapped himself with the expensive and compelling puzzle of the acorn and he would self-destruct completely or fade into petty oblivion before he could let it go.

He gulped the cheap corn whiskey and shuddered. Eddy Horn didn't like expensive things. He would rather suffer than pay extra carbon for almost anything. But there comes a silver moment in the lifecycle of sombunall humans when they will happily pay almost any price to never be forgotten, or at least remembered from time to time. And although Dr. Horn was a middling urgent care doctor, which is not altogether unnotable, he pretended at so much more... Secretly, he would nevertheless agree to pay Jaina whatever rate she requested to get Aaron Waters as his medical research subject.

"Hello?" Jaina queried him, wondering why he was breathing into the receiver disgustingly.

"Alright, well let's go over there and let's get him then. What do you need from me?" he asked her absently.

"Do you have a plane?"

He drained his glass and poured another. He didn't have a plane. But he was owed a favor from someone who did. He would call in his favor from Freedom Vinolte. With what she owed him she couldn't refuse him.

"I can get one."

★   ★   ★

Meanwhile, Aaron Waters marched at spearpoint with his two new sterilized comrades through a thick wood. The Trees lined the well-trodden path in a grid pattern. They must have been planted centuries ago. These were larger than any rumored to be in the American preserves and Aaron hadn't seen even a single blade of fiberweed since he'd been delivered to the strange land of Norwegia.

"I can't believe our hunting trip turned into a slave round-up. It's not fair. We came to hunt mammoths, not geldings," he heard one of the Amazons complain.

"This one has seeds intact and he's unregistered. He may be an invader. It's our duty to turn him over to the authorities in the city. Who knows what diseases he could be carrying? We will all probably have to be quarantined as well. We may be unable to join the festivities of the seasonal delights next week. He's ruined more than just this hunt," another said and spat.

Angered, she gave him a swift slap to the back of the head. Aaron had flown out of the frying pan in the sky and into the fire of this termagant nation of viragoes ... from the clutches of one hunting party: who had meant to disentangle his nervous system from his body and incorporate it into some kind of extraterrestrial network of neurons; to another which was going to erase his manhood and incorporate his body into their extra-testicular network of the neutered.

Aaron could feel forest debris beneath his feet. Leaves and sticks luxuriously crackled under his weight. He inadvertently kicked an acorn a few feet down the path, then bent down and picked it up. The Amazons either didn't notice or more likely they didn't care, and he slipped it into his pocket.

"Where do you think they are taking us?" Aaron asked his new ninny buddies.

"Back to the power plant, I'm sure," one said.

"Back to the grind, the nuclear waste won't sort itself," the other chimed in.

Be that as it may, he was truly thrilled to be in the fresh air and the dappled sunlight of the Amazon's sacred groves. His feet were in chains but he felt somehow freer than he'd ever felt before. And although neither he nor the Amazons knew it, he was once again being hunted.

★   ★   ★

Freedom was in bed but still awake when her tracer lit up. She wanted to let it ring, but the video voicemail feed automatically popped up and Dr. Eddy Horn appeared in living color before her, the last person she wanted to see in her bedroom.

Freedom, it's Dr. Horn. Listen, I need a favor. I need one of your planes. There's this guy I've been looking for … I'm sure you heard about the guy who found an Oak. I've hired someone to find him. And she found him, but he's in Norwegia. Can you believe that? I don't how he got there or how she found him — she's some kind of a technology sorceress.

She picked up.

"She found him? I didn't know he'd gone missing. Look, Eddy. I know you think I owe you something for finding my sister, but I don't want you calling here. I don't know how else to say this, but you are hideous, and your presence as a hologram is somehow even more intolerable than having to endure you in person. And to make it all worse, you're in the middle of my bedroom right now."

"And I apologize. But you're the only person I know with a plane and I thought you might consider lending it to me to resolve the situation with Acorn Waters. Plus, it's not like I can see you. Your vid feed is one way, right? So, what do you say?"

"Whatever. Take my plane and get the guy, but don't call me again. Here's the tracer number of my pilot. And if you find Aaron, be sure you get that acorn from him. If that wild acorn was produced from a fiber-resistant tree then I need its genetics. Talk to my team. Remember: don't call me again, Eddy. And if you're successful, I'll make sure you are remembered for this," she said, finessing his psyche.

"Thanks, Freedom, I truly app-"

Freedom disconnected from the call and turned over in her bed. She was tickled that Dr. Horn was trying to find the acorn guy. She wondered how the generally ineffective doctor would succeed at the task. But she didn't care enough to weather even one moment more of Eddy Horn's image in her magnificent bedroom. Freedom fell backward into her pillow. A person-sized lump revealed itself and rolled over in bed, peaking at her with sky-blue eyes through a mess of blond hair. It was her doppelganger.

"Why risk the plane, and the pilot on this guy? There's no guarantee that hare-brain doctor has any real leads," the other Freedom asked.

"I just want that acorn, Trish. That wild tree could be resistant to your marvelous bugs, or worse: it could be allelopathic to the fiber itself. It could be the worst threat to our business we've ever faced."

"Don't remind me about those microbes. I only agreed to release them because you convinced me it would destroy the fiberweed. Now we're in bed together!"

She cracked a devilish smile at her pun.

"We sure are…"

Freedom turned over and took her twin in an embrace under the covers.

★   ★   ★

Elsewhere, the object of Freedom and Dr. Horn's ire began to settle into his new situation. Aaron Waters never saw the huntresses again after they'd left him in the custody of the nuclear power plant manager. The plant manager was a sturdy woman with stout legs like Tree trunks. She took a special interest in Aaron and gave him easy tasks. He was quickly given a role as a supervisor. He noticed all the other supervisors, of whom there were maybe a dozen, appeared to also be unaltered men, although unlike Aaron they all had pale skin, as did the effeminate workers. The rest were all eunuchs and there were uncountable numbers of them skittering about the giant facilities. He was charged with overseeing more than 100 at a time, which was easy as they mostly kept each other busy by trying to win his favor through backbiting and other petty nonsense.

"Aaron, I mopped the floor. I am the only one who mops the floor around here. It seems, *Sigh* that the other ones are all so lazy. Don't you think?"

It took him less than a week to get the hang of the job. It was easy because very little was expected of him by the management. Aaron enjoyed the routine and being inside every day. He had a cozy place to stay and hadn't missed a meal. He didn't have to commute to work because they all lived under the same power plant. At first, he had hoped that the Magi would rescue him and return him to his home in Florida, USA.

He hadn't given his circumstances much thought since settling in at the power plant. Was it simple traumatization that pushed the bizarre events of his recent past to the periphery of his conscious mind? He was more at home here in the so-called Sisterland of Norwegia. Whatever the case, he had already given up on the possibility of anyone coming to get him. But as he would soon find out, in this regard Aaron had erred.

★   ★   ★

"We're almost there, Jaina," Freedom's pilot told his passenger.

"It says here that the power plant workers of Norwegia are all fixed, and they live like ants in underground barracks. They file up to work in the plants and retire after their shifts to great subterranean halls. They are kept well, but they don't get any animal protein. The neo-Amazons keep all the wild game for themselves," Jaina Shields said from the back seat of the cockpit of the small aircraft reading a book.

"What's that you're looking at? I didn't think anyone knew anything about the Norwegs," the pilot asked her.

"It's a book. It's an old travelogue from before they became a hermit nation. By the way, did you know their shield is *my* design?"

"Yeah, you mentioned that. I just hope the shields you installed on my plane work like you say they will."

"Oh, they will. The ship's shield will merge with the Norweg shield and we will be absorbed, like an amoeba. They won't even notice our arrival."

The pilot grimaced and thought *what has Freedom gotten me into?*

They passed through the shield with a jolt. Jaina shut off the plane's shield emitter as it was now like a drop in an ocean of shield emissions.

"How did you find this guy, anyway? It's not like there's an embassy to call."

"It's easy. You know how the government tracks our movements with our tracers? I just used the government's tracking database. His tracer wasn't in America so I accessed a Russian spy satellite and I found it here in Norwegia. If the Amazons found him, he should be in quarantine. If not, we'll just pick him up from the forest or field or wherever he's hiding," she nonchalantly replied.

"Forest? You can't be serious."

"Of course I am! Apparently, they never got fiberweed. This book says they were trying to re-introduce extinct animal species like wooly mammoths. Their genetic engineering is decades ahead of us in America."

"That's impossible. Everyone knows the USA is the best at everything," the pilot told her.

Jaina looked at her map on which she'd traced Aaron's tracer. It looked like his was in a city amid a vast expanse of forested hills and craggy mountains.

"Just keep flying due east and we should see civilization soon. He's there under their power plant, I'd bet on it."

*   *   *

As she suspected, Aaron was indeed being held captive. Whether he was himself aware of that was something else entirely, but for five weeks now he had been living under the power plant and supervising its workers. Time for him had become a blur. He had forgotten the names of the days, what month, and even which season it was outside.

One afternoon, Aaron's manager offered to have him over after work. He didn't know why she wanted to see him, and he was more than a little nervous. It was a small ordeal for him to get to her apartment, for it was not in the power plant at all but above it and he needed to be escorted there in a special elevator. Once in her apartment, the nuclear Amazon engineer brought out a strange citrus fruit and peeled it near Aaron's forehead, which sprayed Aaron's face with an organic, oily mist. The fragrance triggered a deep nostalgia in him. He was overwhelmed with the feeling of ineffable memory. He thought maybe she had drugged him.

"What is it?" he asked.

"It's an orange. Try it."

In devouring a slice, he gained a sort of fructoid-enlightenment: the orange flavor of the orange beverages from his Florida, USA homeland was based on a fruit named an orange, and not simply because the drink is orange.

I wonder what's the fruit for blue flavor? Aaron thought to himself.

"I have so much else to show you, Aaron," she said warmly.

She took his arm gently. Here hands were strong but soft. She was much larger physically than him and he was somewhat intimidated. Looking around he noticed the furs on the floor, and the bones and skulls on the mantle, and antlers were strewn about the place. *Is she going to devour me?*

She giggled. She wouldn't take her eyes off him. Aaron looked now at her face – her dry cracking lips parted and her straight pearly teeth peeped through with a gleam, her mahogany freckles camped out on her cheeks, her big green eyes peered into his with an inquiry from under the golden curtains of her neatly trimmed bangs. Her smooth forehead was like the hull of a wooden ship, and her sparse eyebrows rose to decipher his emotional state. He felt secure for one of the only times in his life but it made him unsettled. It was too good to be true. *Surely,* a voice from his childhood interjected, *you don't deserve to feel this way.*

"You deserve this, Aaron. We all do," she assured him.

Did she just read my mind? Is she another one of those Magi?

He felt adrenaline release in his belly. He exhaled deeply and stood up. She stood up a second later, her concentration broken.

"Perhaps that is all for now, Aaron. Please be on time again tomorrow."

Even though he no longer had to commute, he was still late once or twice a week. This was the first anyone had mentioned it.

"Of course ... You know, I still don't know your name."

"Yes, Aaron. I know that," she said with a laugh.

"Here, take this," she handed him a card key for the elevator. "Come see me any time you want!"

She closed the door. He was perplexed and over-whelmed, and still hungry after only having a bite of the orange to eat. But there persisted a brilliance behind his eyes and a warmness that lasted within his belly, as if her smile had irradiated his internal organs to a glow. He became aware of it when, after opening the worker entrance to the plant, he smiled for the first time in memory.

★   ★   ★

Jaina Shields and Freedom's pilot descended into a splotch of daffodil sparkles contained in the dusky outlines of an advanced civilization surrounded by darkness and the starry horizon. What she thought was a city turned out to be the power plant itself. The whole thing was part of one massive complex. According to her rough estimation, it could generate way more power than was necessary for just the shields, but what else could they be powering? It hadn't looked like many people lived in Norwegia, at least from what she'd seen so far.

The plane touched down gradually after hovering briefly over an empty parking lot. The entire place seemed deserted on the surface.

Jaina was still confident that she would have no trouble finding Aaron. She called him on his tracer and he picked up on the second ring.

"Hello?"

"Hey Aaron, how's it going?"

"Good, who's this?"

"This is the person who's going to rescue you from Norwegia and bring you home to America. We have a plane outside, just get out of there and let's go."

"Oh, well … That's okay. I like it here. I think I'm gonna stay."

"… Aaron, this is Gloria, Gloria Day. Why don't you come outside and say hi? I've come a long way to see you."

Aaron knew deep down that the person on the other line probably wasn't Gloria. But he also knew he couldn't hang up without making sure. He'd never forgotten Gloria Day, the friendly and competent nurse who had treated his heat exhaustion, and with whom he'd hastily infatuated himself after one phone conversation about jellyfish. Then, suddenly he remembered how he'd gotten to Norwegia: first kidnapped by the aliens outside the Gummy Nugs© outlet, then the magi, and the Valkyries. The thought of someone from his old life coming to visit was comforting, and he allowed himself to begin to believe it could be her.

"Gloria?" he whimpered.

He still didn't fully believe it could be Gloria on the line, but who else could it be? At the very least it was someone who knew enough about him and Gloria to pretend to be her.

Aaron wandered pensively out of his hovel and down the corridor to the service elevator. He rode it up to the lobby of the workers' quarters. There was no one around except a few worn-out workers he didn't recognize. No security was necessary here as escapes were so few and far between. Aaron simply swiped his cardkey at the special elevator, rode it up to the ground floor, and left out the front door. And there she was: a wispy purple-cloaked figure with dangerous angles. He saw the glint of the barrel to her laser pistol in her hip holster. She looked him up and down. He was wearing a silly-looking cap that said *SUPERVISOR* on it.

"Aaron, let's just talk. What are you doing here?"

"You aren't Gloria," he replied obliviously.

"No, I lied. I needed to get you out of there. I can't go in there because I'm not an Amazon. Do you have the acorn? Let's go!"

"Yeah, I've got an acorn, but I won't go back to Florida with you. I like it here. Please don't take me," he said, finally catching on to what was happening.

Jaina drew her pistol.

"Aaron, I need you to come with me. Don't do anything stupid," she said.

"I won't ... What are you going to do, kill me? Whatever," he said stupidly.

He reached into his pocket, grabbed the Norweg acorn he'd kept there for good luck, and tossed it towards Jaina. She saw it roll and bounce on the pavement, finally hitting her foot and coming to a stop. He turned and walked back to the door of the giant power plant complex. Jaina fired her laser over his shoulder, but he didn't turn to look at her. He stopped for a moment and as the green laser beam glanced off a streetlight and flitted into the sky behind a cloud, it briefly lit up the entire vista neon green. He continued walking away. Was Aaron calling her bluff or was he just reckless? Jaina let her pistol sink. She observed him, dumbfounded that she nearly had him in her custody and now he appeared to be simply walking off. As he slowly, solemnly escaped, Jaina tried one last appeal.

"Aaron, these people are keeping you as a slave! They only want you for your sperm, you know."

Maybe she's right, even if she's rude, Aaron briefly considered the possibility but then fresh memories of the night at his manager's apartment flooded him: the orange fruit, the apparent telepathy, and the magical warmth. They could've taken his sperm any time they wanted it, but they didn't. It was he the Amazons wanted, not his body.

Jaina Shields had uncharacteristically made a critical miscalculation in her retrieval gambit. She hadn't apprehended quickly enough that the fear of death could no longer be used to manipulate Aaron Waters. Truly he'd been too desperate for too long.

I should have just shot him with a tranquilizer dart, Jaina realized. But that tactic hadn't fit the psychological profile she'd drawn up for him at the time. Whatever happened before she got to him had changed his psyche. Plus, she knew there would be problems with keeping him captive: if not now, then later when the erudite Dr. Horn would've had to take custody of him. She had come prepared for a rescue mission, but she should've prepared instead for a kidnapping.

Instead of Aaron doing what he was supposed to have given up easily and gone willingly back to Florida. Jaina reluctantly let him walk away, then bent down and picked up the acorn. She watched as Aaron disappeared behind the front door, the door automatically locking shut behind him with a whirr. Around her the streets were empty and the city was dull with the abiotic humming of subterranean electrical generators reverberating on cooling towers. The lights and the structures were for her like an enemy army to which she now had to surrender. She'd lost her main target, but at least she had the acorn.

"At least I got the acorn," she told the pilot, as they prepared to cross back over the shield border in Freedom Vinolte's plane.

"Let's see it," he gestured to her from the helm.

Jaina was palpating the bereted Oak seed, contemplating her almost total failure. She tossed the capped little nut as the plane crossed the threshold of the shield of Norwegia. The pilot caught it and held it out.

"This is mine now. Freedom said I'd get a bonus if I brought it straight to her, and I–"

They watched as the acorn flickered like a dying candle and slipped out of existence entirely. It had been a hologram. More than that, it had been a flawless photo-tactile synthetic acorn experience. It was indistinguishable from a real acorn, and it couldn't exist outside the boundary of the shield generators.

Now Jaina finally understood why they needed so much electrical power in Norwegia. They weren't just generating shields; they were generating an entire alternate reality. Everything about the place, from the Trees and the grass to their impressive animal herds, had been an elaborate simulation.

CHAPTER 18

Dr. Horn poured his first of the day.

The laughing bones of ice in his glass tinkled and cracked like popping knuckles as the room temperature whiskey surrounded them. It was the ice he noticed would accumulate in the freezer where they kept patients' specimens. *Why let it go to waste?* He paid the electricity bill, and he would save where he could. Besides, it was *his* ice after all – plus, the specimens were on the lower shelf, not even close to his precious, frosty accretions. The doctor was sure it was still perfectly good ice, and he regularly hammered it from the sides of the freezer with the same rubber plexor he would use to test reflexes at the knee.

It was Friday afternoon around 4:30. Gloria Day was approaching his office to quit. She walked right in and told him he was incompetent and abused his position of authority. She wouldn't have gone the extra mile, except that she'd already secured employment at a nice suburban nursing home in New Port Richey, and would be starting Monday.

Telling off her abuser didn't result in the desired outcome. Dr. Horn didn't get flustered or embarrassed or even look very uncomfortable at all.

"So that's it?" he asked, "You're just going to leave me with no coverage on Monday?"

Frustrated, and beginning to feel ashamed of herself, Gloria thought about making a scene. She thought about turning over the sloppy desk with the piles of papers and files or throwing his computer out the window, or dumping his disgusting whiskey in his lap and spitting in his face. But she didn't want to get sued, and she knew Eddy Horn was nothing if not a litigious, scheming scoundrel. He was also a coward and a drunk and she knew he was probably half-in-the-bag and might get a kick out of seeing her angry. He might feel some twisted sense of power. She collected herself, smiled, turned, and walked out of his office feeling lighter, her dignity intact. She wouldn't have to look at that old toad again. And she wouldn't have to listen to his awful voicemails or smell his old-man coffee-breath or pretend he wasn't drinking in his office instead of doing his job all afternoon.

In the hall was a girl: a slight girl she'd never seen before, with a royal purple hood and long, greasy blond hair. Normally, Gloria would ask what her business was with Dr. Horn. It was a wonder she got past reception. But it was no longer her concern.

"Your turn. You'd better hurry up; the old toad might croak any minute now."

"He better wait until my check clears. Take it easy, Gloria."

How does she know my name ... ? Gloria scrutinized the mysterious girl in purple as she strode out the exit, onto the blacktop, and into her already-running, already-cooled DV. This wonder gave her a fine distraction from the unpleasantness of her final encounter with Eddy Horn, M.D.

Then, Jaina Shields walked into the stale office and stood before him. After noticing someone was there, he seemed to start closing out of windows on his laptop.

"Sup Eddy?"

"Oh hey, it's you. My best nurse just quit. She called me an incompetent jerk! Can you believe that?"

"Of course I can believe that, Eddy. Look atchyou. Yer a slob! Ya wear a suit that's too big, cuz you won't spend the money on one that fits right. It smells like booze and breath mints in here! Yer entire … universe," she gestured generally, "is repulsive and pathetic."

"How dare you speak to me that way, young lady? I'm the one that hired you, remember?"

"Whatever. Let me tell you about my trip to Norwegia."

"No, hold on a minute. I want to know where you get off, talking to me like I'm some kind of a nobody. I'm a doctor! How did you get in here, anyway?"

"Eddy. Edward. Eduardo. Yew drink too much. Ya gave me the key to the employee entrance, remember?"

He didn't remember that, but he didn't want to look foolish so he stayed silent.

"Anyway look, here's what happened. Aaron's gone native in Norwegia. He doesn't want to come home," she explained.

"I don't care *what* he wants!"

"He escaped. There was nothing I could do."

"Nothing you *could* do? Or nothing you *would* do? You know, since starting this project you have left me completely in the dark. Now you come waltzing in here expecting what, exactly? I'm supposed to pay you for nothing?"

"You've had use of my shield projector this entire time. And, you signed a contract Eddy. In any case, I learned something useful. The acorn Aaron gave me *disappeared* when we left Norwegia."

"It *disappeared...*? How is *that* useful? What am I supposed to do with an invisible acorn and no patient?" he squawked at her, pinkening and shaking with anger.

"Well, if it makes ya feel any better, Freedom's pilot betrayed me and tried to take the acorn before it dissipated. Freedom probably would've taken Aaron, too!" Jaina smiled brightly and tried mightily to fight off a laugh, but it came out stronger:

"...haHA!"

"You know, for someone who wants to get paid, you are acting awfully disrespectful. I don't feel any services have been rendered. I don't feel I should pay you at all!"

Even a drunk Dr. Horn could get pious when money was on the line.

"Well, you can feel however you want to, but I took the liberty of charging your card for services rendered so you've already paid me. You still need to pay Freedom for her pilot's time and jet fuel but that's between you two. And I guess that's that. Oh, the other thing is that you're paying rent on the shield I gave you until you mail it back to me. The address is printed on the bottom. Thanks. Do you need anything else?"

"Need anything else? Yeah, how's about you get the fuck out of my office? Asshole."

"Hmm, 'k."

She turned to leave and noticed the vein in his forehead was bulging. There was sweat on his forehead now. Dr. Horn felt that charging his credit card was a personal attack, and now his anger consumed him.

Dr. Horn grasped the coffee mug from that morning and hurled it at Jaina's head. Even though she could've dodged it, she didn't feel like giving him the satisfaction of watching her move at his command, so she let her shield do the work. The mug stopped soundlessly in the air and tumbled to the office floor. As the shards settled impotently on the floor of the stuffy office, Jaina didn't break stride. Dr. Horn would never see her again.

Miss Shields had hardly left when the intercom rang. Dr. Horn had begun to get up to look for a dustpan but he sat back down and pushed the button to answer it.

"Hello? This is Dr. Horn."

"Hi Dr. Horn, this is Ruby Schofield with the Bureau of Efficiency in Government. How are you?"

"I've been better, Ruby. What can I do for you?"

"I'm looking for Tricia D'Aster. Do you know where I can find her?"

"Never heard of her," he lied.

"No? Freedom Vinolte, her identical twin, told me to ask you since you were the one administering the twins experiment."

"Freedom told you that?"

That rat.

"Yes, she said that Tricia was her twin and you separated them at birth. Did you get any results or come to any conclusions regarding your experiments? And please explain to me what was the scope of these experiments anyway?"

"Alright, Jesus Christ. Just have the front desk attendant escort you to my office and we'll talk about it."

As Ruby Schofield entered the doctor's office, Dr. Horn leaned back at his desk. He poured himself another drink.

This is it. It's all over. Everyone is going to know about the twins. Gloria is gone. Jaina's got the rest of my money. Aaron and his acorn aren't coming back. There's nothing left to lose.

"Here I am! So enchanted to *finally* meet you, Dr. Horn. Thank you *so* much for taking the time to talk. So, tell me what sort of results did you get from your experiments on twins?"

"Nothing of significance. There were no correlations or conclusions. The sample size was too small. And once the twins discovered each other, the whole thing was blown open. What could I do?"

"So, you killed the poorer twins?"

"What? No! Is that what this is about? Who died?"

"Well, no one that I know of. I just can't account for the whereabouts of Tricia D'Aster."

"Why the hell would you need to? You said you're with BEG? How is that even your business?"

It was never her purview; he was right. Scho' had no defensible reason for asking him these questions. It all went back to her boredom at work and her anger at her boss having asked her to stop using her nickname. If she were going to get anything useful out of him, Ruby would have to get personal. She suddenly remembered the parting words of Dr. Wong from the Wiggle Room.

"It's not my personal business, sir. But the bureau is putting together an article about the *life*'s works of incredibly efficient government scientists. We wanted to finish your file before you *died*," she lied.

"Oh, well I guess I didn't realize you had a file on me. Well yes, it was an efficient study. And very interesting as to what became of Tricia," the spirit of whiskey in Dr. Horn began dribbling words from his mouth.

Oh, just keep talking! Scho hoped, listening wistfully into her phone.

"I guess you can say she became Free," he paused with a whiskey twinkle in his eye, "I had her social security number deleted and she just assumed Freedom's identity. They both agreed that it was the best course of action. They could get more done together and – hey! I guess you could say it was the most efficient way of concluding the study and keeping it a secret, too."

"So, Freedom is actually … two people?"

"Yes, isn't it remarkable? You can absolutely put that down in your article. The first individual that's comprised of two persons: isn't that groundbreaking? I would say so!"

Doctor Horn's prior melancholy had been inverted into baseless enthusiasm after Scho's artful fibs regarding Dr. Horn's noteworthiness and a forthcoming imaginary BEG article about government scientists. With liquor performing as an unexpected solvent, she'd successfully extracted the truth regarding the whereabouts of Tricia D'Aster. She realized there was a 50-50 chance she'd already spoken with the rogue scientist and apparent corporate executive formerly known as Tricia. But what could she *do* with the truth? Expose her? Expose her to whom? Would the police care? Maybe the news would run a story ... Ruby Schofield's head spun with the possibilities. But she wasn't optimistic. It was a tailspin of doubt more than a whirlwind of joy. Regardless, she had finally put the pieces together just like her namesake enzyme. She remembered something that wonderful stranger Dr. Wong had said the other evening at the Wiggle Room:

"Apply the keys to magic and science in equal measure: one key is observation and the other is intention," he seemed to be saying to her in living color from her memory.

...Magic and science in equal measure... the words echoed in her head again.

Then the generous little geomancer faded from her mind and she was left with precious little time to ponder her intentions based on her observations in the office of Dr. Wong's polar opposite, Dr. Horn. Ruby was able to make an exit after a brief exchange.

"Well, I suppose I must be going. Thanks for clearing all of this up, Dr. Horn."

As the young lady left his office, Dr. Horn wondered if they couldn't have conducted that business over the phone. But since this was something he often wondered throughout the course of a day, he was left to tie up his affairs, drunk and alone once again, in his dismal Friday doctor's office.

CHAPTER 19

"The creation of a thousand forests is in one acorn."
—Ralph Waldo Emerson

The Florida DoP employees had plans to meet before dawn at the gas station and drive miles into the fiber. As such, Buck retired that evening to his modest trailer in preparation for the hunting trip. After a couple of straight whiskeys, he had nothing but big country grasshoppers on his mind. He'd shot plenty of nymphs, even a few in their 4th and 5th stage, but he'd never even *seen* an adult. He'd always coveted a trophy of spurs from the hind legs of an adult male giant grasshopper. He remembered seeing a pair of the ruby red and turquoise-dotted razor-sharp leg armors. He tried to recall where. *Was it? ... It couldn't be.* An image of the iridescent haunches of a giant grasshopper: a trophy resultant of two-dozen years haunting the thick fiber. It hung over the giant black walnut slab table in the boardroom of Freedom Vinolte's Mondow Corp. How did he know this? Buck couldn't remember.

He realized he couldn't make sense of any memory before the moment he bought the iStone™. Buck put his drink down and gazed upon the precious pebble. He tried to reminisce again but instead the dullness of a headache came on. He decided he could afford to turn in a little early and hit the hay. That evening he dreamed of a forested landscape containing strange elephantine cattle and the massive women who hunted them into existence. He dreamed he was bound in servitude to these giant women, who didn't allow their men to hunt.

The next morning Ralph Burgman decided he, Pete Barbour, and Joey Dimanche would all ride together out to hunt hoppers in the DoP work truck. As they drove deep into the fibersea, they began to pass the rubble of old condos, houses, and trailers claimed by thick swathes of fiber. The road turned from pavement to gravel, and finally to muddy tracks through hip-high fiber. They parked the truck where it refused to drive any farther in the mud.

Pete said: "Look, the fiber's all chewed-up!"

The three of them took note of all the damage from the hungry hoppers. It could be from a swarm of regular old locusts, but still, they got the sense that any number of giant grasshoppers could fly in at any second.

"I hope I get a shot at one with big spurs. They sell for quite a bit of carbon on Google, you know," Ralph said to his friend and co-worker.

"Yep. You know how I've been trying to build my business mowing lawns?" Pete started to tell a story; "well last year this guy didn't call me but once for the whole year. His fibergrass was up to my neck. Before I turned around to tell him it's too tall to cut with my mower, I scared up this absolute *beast* of a grasshopper. It must have been four feet, not counting the feelers. The spurs must have been at least this long," he gestured out about a foot.

"It flew away faster than I could even think about trying to catch it. I could feel the wind from its wings!"

"Hey, you ever try that ad visor that pays you to wear it?"

"Yeah, but I don't think you could pay me enough to watch ads for money. It comes out to less than minimum wage."

"There's got to be a way to fool it into thinking you're wearing it," Ralph mused.

"Joey, you wore one for about a month. You remember that?" Pete laughed.

"Yeah, I—"

"Yeah, he wouldn't shut up about laundry detergent and basketball sneakers. It didn't make sense. Joey, you would verbatim recite the ads. I started telling him he's gotta start paying us to listen to him spout that nonsense in the truck. I think you were under some kind of mind control," Ralph said in a serious tone.

"It wouldn't be out of the ordinary for this boy. Remember the scheme about the social block-chain dividends? Joey, you swore we would all be rich. And then you had to borrow money for gas and food for a week until you got paid again. I swear, you spend more on those vape pens than I do for rent," Pete said, looking into the distance for hoppers.

"You guys make me sound like a sucker," Joey said, looking forlorn.

Joey sullenly got out of the backseat of the work truck and closed the door pathetically. The light in the truck stayed on because the mechanism didn't take.

"For Christ's sake Joey," Burgman scolded him.

Burgman walked over to the backseat door of the truck, opened it, and quickly slammed it shut. Aaron's acorn had still been squirreled away in the door but it shook loose and into the fertile mud. No one noticed.

The three of them moved slowly over the grazed fiberweed, trying to spot the hoppers before they were seen. Then they heard a car horn honk twice back near where they parked the truck.

"Guess Buck finally made it," Ralph said.

"Should we double back and meet him?" Pete asked.

"Yeah, I reckon we ought to."

Buck piled out of his truck and grabbed his crossbow. He looked at the iStone™ shimmering in the passenger seat. He decided to take it along for the hunt, thinking maybe it would bring luck. As soon as the coveted pebble dropped into his pocket, he heard rustling past the tall fiber. He could see movement. He nocked a bolt and drew his crossbow. He would shoot the hopper as soon as it appeared.

"Hey, Buck! Oh, Jesus. Take it easy, man," Pete Barbour called out as he, Ralph, and Joey appeared from behind the brush.

It was almost too late, but Buck let down his crossbow and put the bolt safely back in his quiver.

"It's a good thing you guys don't have leg spurs," Buck quipped.

"Yeah, I thought you were gonna smoke me!" Joey said, visibly shaken.

"You guys seen any yet? I just pulled up. Looks like there's plenty of sign," Buck remarked, kicking the chewed-up fiber underfoot.

"No, we was just walking around a bit. Saw some grazing but – wait, you hear that?"

The three of them stopped speaking to listen. A soft hum yielded to a louder sort of buzz, and soon a swarm of hoppers was quickly descending upon them. All three readied their arrows and drew their bows.

"Hang on, wait for them to start landing!"

The dozen or so mature hoppers began to flutter down into the clearing to feed. As soon as one landed, it received an arrow right through the thorax. Soon another landed and got the same treatment. The rest of the swarm caught on and aborted their landing. Buck was the only one that hadn't fired yet. He steadied his aim and shot one right out of the air. The giant hopper kicked and thrashed, foaming bloody red syrup from its mouthparts. Dust and fiber particles were sent into the air as the huge insect finished its death spasms.

Buck's dream from the other night was playing out right before his eyes.

"Holy hell!" Ralph said with a hoot and a holler.

★   ★   ★

Jane Franklin had begun to close her store when the purple-hooded silhouette of a familiar lass appeared.

"Sup?" the fay, golden-haired customer greeted the shopkeeper.

"Afternoon, Ms. Shields."

"Did ya know yer shopfront was fake? It ain't a real foyer neither. It was last week, but ain't no more," the young woman informed the purveyor of vapors.

Jane couldn't understand what Ms. Shields was trying to tell her. *Of course it's real, as real as anything else ...* She thought.

"It's plastic, is that what you mean?"

"No, it's holographic. It used to be plastic, and now it's a hologram. Seems like everything is turning into holograms lately, ya notice that?"

Jane Franklin hadn't noticed. She didn't know whether to believe Jaina, the holographic shields specialist and private investigator, or whether her dear customer and friend had lost her marbles.

"Well, Jaina. I will say I've never seen you wrong about something before. So, if you say it's holographic, I'll believe you. But I just don't know how that can be so," Jane told her.

"Oh well. The reason I came by is cuz the vape you sold me a year ago crapped out. Remember your last place in

Tarpon Springs? What a dump that was, this store is much nicer," she said, looking around.

Jaina handed over the dead vape. Jane inspected it for a moment and threw it in the trash.

"Yeah, it looks like it's done. That thing is full of tar. What are you using this for, anyway?"

"What the hell do ya think? Vaporizing stuff! Maybe not the same stuff yer putting in those cartridges of yers. 'Stickyfruit Juicecake'? What the fuck is a 'stickyfruit'? Honestly Jane. Anyway, I'll just buy a new one. I just finished a job so I'm flush with cash," Jaina confided.

She conducted her business and Jane put Jaina's freshly minted carbon in the register. Then Jane watched as Jaina walked out, or rather through, the holographic doors as her shield canceled out the holograms before her like the sea for Moses. *She's always got a shield up,* Jane thought to herself. *Then again, don't we all...*

She locked the front door. Jaina was only her second customer that day. It was she and that other fellow earlier in the day: she thought back and remembered he said his name was Mark Tunnowitz or something ... *Oh well,* she thought. *So ends another week of slow sales. I wonder where all my return customers have gone? Jaina was the first regular I've seen in quite a while ...*

Jane Franklin sighed and turned out the lights. She hit her vape and shuffled through the store, locking the back door behind her on the way out.

Author Bio

Kindred Stockton is the nom de plume of Geoffrey S. Bok. He's an analytical chemist and outdoorsman living with his wife in his hometown of Collinsville, Connecticut: a place where axes were ground and shipped all over the world from the Collins Company. Deep Shade is his first novel and also his first published work of fiction.

Made in the USA
Coppell, TX
15 August 2021

60537930R00142